VATICAN BLOODBATH

by

Tommy Udo

ATTACK! IS AN IMPRINT OF CREATION BOOKS

First published in 2000 by ATTACK! Books
www.creationbooks.com

Design by Rom
Original artwork by Paul McAffery
Printed and bound in Great Britain by
Woolnough Bookbinding Ltd
Irthlingborough, Northants

ATTACK! wishes to make it perfectly clear that *VATICAN BLOODBATH* is a work of avant-pulp FICTION set in an ALTERNATIVE universe very DIFFERENT from our own,

None of the characters are intended to resemble any living person.

All the other members of the FICTIONAL British Royal Family in VATICAN BLOODBATH are NOT intended in any way, shape or form to be representations or caricatures of yer *ACTUAL* British Royal Family.

No Way. We love our Queen. Gawd bless her.

Also published by **ATTACK!** books

Satan! Satan! Satan! by Tony White

Raiders Of The Low Forehead by Stanley Manly

Tits-Out Teenage Terror Totty by Steven Wells

Get Your Cock Out by Mark Manning and

Whips & Furs: My life as a Gambler, Bon Vivant and Love Rat by Jesus H. Christ
(edited and introduced by Stewart Home)

AND COMING SOON....

Bloody Heroes by Bob Morris

Tokyo Bloodbath 2002 by Stanley Manly and

Ebola 3000 by Richard Marshall

All *ATTACK!* books can be ordered for £6.99 each from
www.creationbooks.com
or
Creation Books 4th Floor, City House,
72-80 Leather Lane London EC1N 7TR

Tommy Udo left his job in a Glasgow steelworks to follow The Smiths around Britain in a hearse. He drove up and down outside the venues throwing root vegetables at the queuing fans while blasting them with extreme heavy metal.

Then he got God, was received into the Catholic Church and trained to become a priest but soon realised that it was all bollocks. Then he got a job at Balmoral as a gamekeeper but was soon sacked for what was officially described by a palace official as "over-familiarity".

After a brief stint as a pro-wrestler he became Britain's top cyber-journalist.

He lives in London and does not take any drugs of any description any more.
This sometimes makes him a bit grumpy.

(This page has been left blank so you can use your crayons to draw a picture of Tommy strangling a fox for the Queen.)

“The signs that will precede the second coming of Christ will be identified by unprecedented war, revolution, drought, famine, pestilence, plagues of the most hideous kinds, earthquakes, violence, death and especially crime and sin unparalleled in human history, and that Christ warned us that in those days sin and evil will abound in the world and that the love of truth will grow cold.
In the mid-fifties, Pope Pius XII said that there was more sin being committed then than at any other time in human history, even before the Great Flood. This statement was made before (the) abortion, homosexuality and child abuse which is so rampant today.”

Advertisement online for amateur video
The Rise of The Anti-Christ

(http://www.catholictreasures.com/descrip/30121.html)

PROLOGUE 1:

UPSTAIRS IN A BAR, SOMEWHERE IN ROMAN OCCUPIED JUDEA, 33 AD

"I'm back," said Yeshua Ben Joseph aka Big Jesus aka Jerusalem Slim, slamming his sword on the table. "And this time I've brought a sword!"

The disciples started giving each other high fives and whooping and hugging each other and saying "Alright!"

"Man, how the fuck did you escape?" asked Thomas. "They, like, hammered nails into your hands and shit."

Jesus held up his wrists and showed him the holes.

The disciples nodded knowingly.

"Man, that's *gotta* hurt!" said one of the Simons.

"Can I, like, just check you out, man?" said Thomas, poking his finger into one of the holes. "Not that I, like, doubt you or anything, dude."

"Hey, whatever..." said Jesus. "But check this shit out. I gots me someone here y'all gonna want to talk to. Hey Jude! C'mon in."

Judas Iscariot walked through the door with a big shit-eating grin on his face.

"What the fuck.!" gasped John.

"Be cool, bitches," said Jesus, throwing an arm around Judas's shoulders, "be cool!"

"But Jesus, man," said Frank (one of the disciples who has since been written out of the true history) "that cocksucker sold you out, man. He went and like rolled over for the fucking Romans, dude!"

"He's like a snitch, man," said Barnabas of South Central Samaria.

Yeah, man," said Philip, "let's do the bitch and send, like, his balls back to his momma!"

Jesus held up his holy hands for some shutting the fuck up.

"Whoa," he said. "Judas here is my man."
They gave each other big props.
"What y'all ladies don't realise is that Judas here was acting on my behalf," said Jesus. "I told Judas to go to the Romans and tell them that he would pimp-kiss me in exchange for immunity and a small cash gratuity."
Judas threw a handful of silver coins on the table.
"Now, how about one of you motherfuckers goes and gets us some of that good-shit wine they got downstairs and not this po' nigga shit that y'all sittin' here drinkin?" laughed Jesus.
"But, man..." said Simon Peter, knocking the palms of his hands against his forehead, his eyes screwed shut in confusion. "Why. The. Fuck. Would. You . Do This. *Shit?* Faking your own death...setting us up like that?"
Jesus smiled and clapped his hands on the disciple's shoulder.
"We got a lot of stuff to do," he said. "A lot of RIGHTEOUS stuff. We gots to kick the motherfuckin' Romans out. Am I right?"
There were choruses of "damn straight!" And "fuckin' A!" from around the room.
"And then what? We go back to gettin' ruled by some Jew kings and priests and shit? Some rich Jew fucker instead of some Roman fucker telling us what to do?" Jesus looked around. "We go back to pretendin' that we is the chosen race? That Mr Lord Fucking God All Fucking Mighty is on our side?"
There were murmurs of "no" and "fuck that shit".
"Mah brothers," said Jesus, picking up the rhetoric that wowed the crowds all over Judea and scared the crap out of the Romans and their establishment lickspittles. "Kicking out the Romans is only the start. We have to take this fight all over the world, to the po' oppressed folks of Gaul an' Greece an' Britannia and - yeah - even into the heart of Rome itself. We got to kick out all the priests and the fat-assed merchants here at home. But we also gots to kick 'em out all over the world. Y'all remember the shit I said about the needles and how it's

easier for camels to pass through them than for rich folks to be righteous? Remember all that stuff about loving your neighbour? Well, your neighbour isn't just the guy who lives next door and screws his wife too loud on workday mornings and borrows your best gourd and don't give it back and throws his trash into your back garden. Your neighbour is the woman in Samaria getting stoned because of some arbitrary rich-folks' law say she's a ho. Your neighbour is the slave boy who gots to suck Roman dick cos his ass is a different colour. Hell, your neighbour is the citizen of Rome that's trying to do the right thing while all those sick twisted rich fucks around him go 'bout humpin' little kids and watchin' folks fightin' to the death to get their kicks. An' you gots to love our neighbour, cos that's the only way we're gonna build a world fit for folks to live in."

The disciples started banging on the table, applauding uproariously, jumping to their feet. Judas mouthed "You the man!" and pointed both fingers at Jesus. Simon Peter came to him, hesitated and then threw his arms around him. The applause went on for nearly ten minutes before Jesus calmed it down.

"Now this shit ain't gonna be easy and there's gonna be a lot of folks against us. Powerful folks with big deep purses. That's why I can't afford any ambiguity. That's why we go to get the message across loud and clear," he said. "Now me and Judas have worked out a strategy. We call this new world order "socialism", on account of how folks needs to be more sociable to get along. And the way we go about this is by building a mass movement with a trained and disciplined cadre of professional revolutionary leaders..."

The disciples began making notes and listening intently. Suddenly the door burst open and in walked Saul (nee Paul) of Tarsus accompanied by a detachment of Roman soldiers and some plain-clothes Pharisees.

"OK!" Barked Saul (nee Paul). "Tax Office! Everyone is under arrest. Stay exactly where you are and nobody gets hurt."

"FUCK YOU, PIG!" said one disciple, grabbing his sword and whacking the head offa Roman Centurion.
Suddenly the room was soon a whirl of swishing metal, severed limbs and gushing arteries. Jesus reached for his sword and confronted Saul (nee Paul).
"So, we meet at last," smirked the Roman collaborator.
"You can't win," said Jesus calmly. "You can't kill an idea. You can stop us now, but soon others will arise and your kind will be beaten."
The thin lipped taxman smiled and raised his sword.
Jesus fixed him with his eyes and put his own sword down in front of him (exactly like Obi Wan Kenobi in the first Star Wars).
"Die, you black commie bastard!" screamed Saul (nee Paul) hacking the saviour in two with one cut of his heavy blade.

After the carnage was over, the survivors were led away.
"Bring the body of their leader," ordered Saul (nee Paul). "We can't afford to leave any relics."
"Sir!" barked the Roman soldier, giving him an upright right-handed salute.
"And let me speak to these two," he indicated a badly scarred and beaten Judas and a scared looking Peter.
They were frog marched before him.
"Well, well," sneered Saul (nee Paul). "What have we here? Tell me, you don't actually believe all that crap about building a world based on equality and love do you? You have other reasons for being involved, am I right?"
Judas spat in his face.
"Your kind will never understand, pig!" he snarled defiantly.
Saul (nee Paul) smiled, took a small sharp knife from his pocket and slit Judas's throat from ear to ear.
Judas collapsed, hissing "I forgive you, pig!" through the bloody froth that bubbled forth form his already purpling lips.
Then the tax man turned to Peter.
"And you? What do you have to say?"

"I...I w-w-was only o-o-o-obeying o-o-o-orders!" stammered the cowardly apostle.
"And what were these orders, little man?" asked Saul (nee Paul).
"We were to go and preach the message all over the world and build an unshakeable party organisation dedicated to liberty and equality, to fight oppression (whether economic, sexual, racial or political) wherever it arose. We were to spread the teachings of Jesus and develop theory of our own to deal with the situation as it arose...We were to make converts at all levels of society from slaves to patricians, in the army and in the civil service. And then we would bring about the Kingdom of Heaven on Earth." gabbled the coward.
"Hmmm," said Saul. "Almost like one of these mad religions we hear so much about in Rome. Mithraism or the Isis Cult, perhaps?"
"Except without the magic and miracles," said Peter. "Jesus said that he was a son of God, but that everyone was a son or daughter of God. God, of course, being a metaphor for the commonwealth of humanity and the universe."
Saul (nee Paul) nodded sagely and pondered for a moment.
"You know, Peter," he said slimily, "that isn't such a bad idea. A religion, I mean, organised on the cell structure that Jesus had planned. It needs work, of course...a more realistic goal that the Kingdom Of Heaven..."
He paused again.
"Peter, how would you like a chance to live?" he smiled.
"Oh, yes sir!" beamed the grateful, dog-like former fisherman. "What do I have to do?"
"What I want you to do, Peter, is to go ahead and set up this...let us call it a Church, shall we? And spread the news about Jesus...or at least some of it," he said. "I want you to be the leader of this movement. Its patriarch, its...papa, if you like. Or even...its pope. Yes, that's it. You'll be the first pope of this church."
"Oh thank you thank you!" he grovelled.

"Naturally, I will be in control," said Saul (nee Paul). "But you were one of Jesus's posse. People know you. Peter, you'll be a great front man. Guard! Untie him!"
Peter fell to his knees and began to kiss the feet of Saul (nee Paul).
"That's an audacious move, sir," said a thin, reptilian Roman officer who had overheard the conversation. "Why on Earth would you want to do this thing?"
"Oh," said the sly Saul (nee Paul), "let's just say that the Roman Empire in its present form won't last forever. Jesus was right. Sooner or later some other demagogue would come along and turn the poor against their rightful masters with some dream of an egalitarian society. I think we need to make contingency plans now to both preserve the Roman Empire and to set up an ideological bulwark against these ludicrous ideas whenever they arise in the future. People need to be kept in their place. And what better way to do that than with a religion?"
"Very clever, sir," smirked the Roman. "I salute you. What do we do with the rest of the survivors?"
"Kill all the women first," ordered Saul (nee Paul) with a shudder. "Urgh...the thought of all their vile mucal...secretions from their...*holes*..."
He retched.
"You don't like girls, do you Peter?" Saul asked the grovelling lapdog at his feet. "Nasty, hairy...*wet* things! "
"What about the rest?"
"Those who are not with us are against us," he said. "And they get killed, just like their precious Jesus!"
"Sir!" barked a Roman soldier. "Begging your pardon, sir. But the one you wanted us to find. The body of Jesus, that is, sir...well it's..."
"Yes? What is it, man?"
"It's...*gone*, sir!"
Saul (nee Paul). shook his head.
Not again!

THE PROLOGUE TO THE PROLOGUE

In the closing years of the second millennium, the Great Secret War reached its bloody climax.

Ever since Henry VIII sacked the monasteries, the English Monarchy and the Holy Roman Empire have been at war.

In the early 80s a brainwashed Hashishim Assassin, paid for covertly by British Gold, had attempted to assassinate Pope John Paul II.

The Vatican responded in 1984 by trying to blow up the English puppet government through their agents within the IRA.

The Pope hastily visited the Queen and sued for a truce after she threatened to sign a secret pact with Ayatollah Khomeni to turn Britain into an Islamic fundamentalist state.

The Pope, being the dumb cunt that he was, took her seriously and reasoned that it wasn't in Rome's best interest to have a bunch of mad Mussies on Europe's doorstep.

Islam, he knew, was like a bad flu, hence the Vatican's covert and enthusiastic support for the Croat fascists during the Bosnian war.

They had struggled over control of the slave trade in the Americas - a struggle that the British had all but lost - and had been battling over control of the opium, heroin and cocaine markets for over 100 years.

The Vatican-backed Sicilian Mafia had all but cornered the market in the 1970s and '80s.

The Queen's back was against the wall and she was no longer going to take things lying down.

Now read on...

‘The Pope is not only the representative of Jesus Christ, but he is Jesus Christ Himself, hidden under the veil of the flesh. Does the pope speak? It is Jesus Christ who speaks. Does the Pope accord a favour or pronounce an anathema? It is Jesus Christ who accords the favour or pronounces that anathema. So that when the pope speaks we have no business to examine.’

Pope Pius IX while Archbishop Of Venice

Quoted in *Is Not The Church of Rome The Babylon Of The Book of Revelation?*
An essay by Christopher Wordsworth, DD.

PROLOGUE 2:

THE COURT OF HENRY VIII, ENGLAND, THE SIXTEENTH CENTURY

The Pope’s envoy trembled as Henry VIII advanced on him, fists clenched like two haunches of roast mutton, his pork-pie face contorted with raw hate and rage.
“What the fuck are you saying, ya cunt?”
“H...h...his Holiness regrets that he cannot in all conscience grant you an annulment,” said the quaking cardinal, all ponced up in his purple finery and reeking of perfumed water and hair oil.
“You get tae fuck!” spat the fat king towering over the priest. “Ah’m gonnae knock your fuckin’ block off, ya cheeky wee

shite!"
"Haud on, Hen," said Sir Thomas More positioning himself between the King and the Papal Envoy. "The wee man here's just daein' his joab. Ye cannae take it out on him."
"Aye," said Cardinal Wolsey. "Gie the cunt a brek, your majesty."
"Ah'll gie him a fuckin' brek awright," thundered the king. "Ah'll brek his fuckin' neck! Then ah'll snap his heid aff and shag the hole in his fuckin' neck! Ye hear that, ya wee shite!"
Chancellor and best pal restrained the King who was shaking with spasms of white hot anger.
"You, sonny Jim, had better get yer fuckin' arse back tae Rome ASA fuckin' P an' tell that cunt o' a Pope tae think again," said Wolsey, stabbing his pudgy index finger into the Envoy's pigeon chest. "Christ, pal, are you fuckin' styoopit comin' in here an' tellin' Big Hen that he cannae get a divorce?"
"She's an ugly auld boot!" thundered the King. "Ah've no' even shagged her yince. Ah want tae marry mah new bird!"
"B...b...but the Pope's already given you a divorce once," stammered the Envoy.
"HEY!" bawled the king, straining to attack the Envoy. "EVERY CUNT MAKES MISTAKES, OK PAL?"
"But why is it so important to get married? I mean, we can be very understanding if he just wants to knob her on the side...some Hail Marys, a donation to the coffers..."
"Ah want a wee baby boy," said the king, breaking down in tears. "A wee boy of my own tae play at fitba' wi' and..."
The rest was lost in a loud wail of sobs and choking on snot and tears.
Sir Thomas Moore rolled his eyes.
"Now see what you've done," said Wolsey, shaking his head. "There, there son, don't you cry. We'll get ye a wee boy, don't you worry yersel'."
"WAAAAAAAAARRRRRRRGGGGGGGGGHHHHH HHHHHHH!" howled the king.

"You get tae fuck, right?" said Wolsey. "And don't bang the door on the way back tae Rome."
Wolsey and Moore left the king sobbing his heart out on the throne. They passed Anne Boeleyn in the corridor.
"Whit's aw' the shouting?" she asked.
"Aw, eh, the Pope willnae gie Big Hen a divorce," said Wolsey.
"Aw aye, ah've heard that yin before," she said. "Men! They're aw' the fuckin' same. Promise ye the Earth but, when it comes the time, they never leave their wives. 'The Pope willnae gie us a divorce, dear'. Christ, if I had a groat for every time some smooth talkin' shitebag's said that tae us..."
"Look, dear, me an' Tam here are awa' tae sort it out," said the Cardinal. "You away in there an' try tae calm the big daft bastard doon a bit. He disnae need ony o' yer lip."
"Aye, awright," she grinned. "Ah know whit he needs right now."
She popped out her wooden teeth and mimed giving a slow blow job.
"Oh, naughty!" laughed the Cardinal, wagging his finger.
"Oh aye, an' you would know, too," she chided.
"Oh, I don't know what you mean!" he said in mock indignation. "I'm a celibate priest, you know."
"Aye, celibate for five minutes every day!" She shrieked with laughter as she went into the royal chamber.
Moore and Wolsey laughed too. Once she was gone, Wolsey muttered: "Fuckin' lippy cow. She's gaun the right way tae ge her fuckin' heid whacked aff."
Moore nodded.
"But listen," he said. "The Pope isnae gannae come through wi' Big Hen's divorce."
"Aw ah know" said Wolsey shaking his head. "Stubborn auld fucker. Ah'm fucked if I know whit tae dae."
"Well, look, you're a fuckin' Cardinal, pal," said Moore. "Ye've just got tae tell him that he's got tae live wi' it. Ah mean, it's the fuckin' Pope we're talking aboot here, not the Duke o' Fuckinghamshire. I mean, where do yer loyalties lie?"

"Well look at it this way," said Wolsey. "What's the fuckin' Pope ever done for us?"
"Hey haud oan," said Moore. "That's Protestant talk, pal."
"Ah'm just sayin'..." shrugged Wolsey.
"Look, the Pope's being a right cunt about this, but ye cane just go an' turn Protestant as soon as ye don't agree. Ye'd end up wi' a fuckin' reformation on yer hands."
"Look, Tam, I'm the first tae admit that the Roman Catholic Church has served those of us in the power elite well over the past 1500 years or so, but times are changing. The Vatican cannae haud ontae power forever an' maybe we should be in on the ground floor of something else. Listen, thae cunts in Rome are saft as shite. Ye saw that mincin' wee pansy that the Pope sent? A bunch o' fuckin' arse bandits an' dug rapists the lot o' them. Aw's ahm sayin' is that if ye're gannae keep the plebs in line ye're gannae need mair than a few wee fairies in the pulpit blabbin' away at them in Latin. Christ, it isnae sae long ago that we had a fuckin' peasants' revolt here. Remember tha' Wat Tyler cunt? We need tae look at ither options," said Wolsey.
"Aw ah'm sayin' nothin'," said Moore. "Ah canne fuckin' believe whit ah'm hearing."
"Suit yersel', Tommy Boy, but I think that Big Hen's gonnae see things my way when all's said and done," shrugged Wolsey, walking off leaving Moore quaking with a mix of fear and bile.
"Fuckin' fat cunt!" he spat. In Latin.

The next day Cardinal Wolsey was found mysteriously snuffed in his study.
Big Hen went apeshit.
"It's no fer! Aw a want is a wee sonny boy o' mah ain an' noo mah fuckin' pal's deid," he raged and stormed. "God's a cunt, so he is."
"Heh, yer majesty," said one of the other courtiers, a man named Thomas Cromwell. "There's a fellah here frae Germany tae see ye. Says he's a Proddy or something."

"Oh aye?" said the King. "Whit does he want?"
A sour faced kraut dressed in black and carrying a big heavy leather-bound book entered and stood erect to attention, a look of mad fanaticism in his eyes.
"King Henriech the Eighth?" he said. "Ich bin ein Protestant. Ein kamerad of Martin Luther's. Ve heard you ver having some trouble viz zer Pope. Thought you might be interested in zis NEW! IMPROVED! religion from Chermany."
"Aye, well, erm, ah'm a wee bit busy right now..."
"Look, mein Kaiser, with Protestantism zere's no more kow-towing in zer direction of Rome. If you vant you can start your own church," said the German Prod. "You vant a divorce? Ve haf no problem viz zat. Get divorced as many times as you like. You vant to use reliable contraceptives when they finally get invented? Fine viz us."
"Och, I dunno..."
The German looked around conspiratorially.
"Look, I'm not supposed to tell you zis but...ach, himmel, I like you, sir. Vat I heard vaz zat zer Pope vaz going to give you zer divorce and had written zer letter and just as he vaz about to sign it, his dog bit his balls and knocked his ink-vell over and he couldn't be bothered writing it all out again..."
"WHIT!!!!???"
"That's vat I heard," shrugged the German. "And anuzzer thing...the Church has schtopped your people turning zer profit by lending money at interest, hence zer Chews, sir, the Christ-killers zemselves, now dominate zis trade. Get into Protestantism on zer ground floor and you could vun day not only heff your own church, but your own bank! You could be rich as zer fuck, mein herr!"
"Fuck it!" the King raged. "If the Pope wants tae fuck with me, let him come and fuckin' try it tae mah face! Ah'm a fuckin' Proddy no!."
Sir Thomas Moore just shrugged.
"Aye well fuck you too, pal," screamed the meaty monarch. "OK, ya cunts, lets see some action! You you and you! Get

some cunts tigither and get out there and sack the monasteries. Get us some gold, eh? We'll get it made intae some nice plates tae eat wur dinner aff. You and you, away and form us a new church called...fuck knows...the Church of England, with me at the head of it. Get the Scots tae start wan tae, except even mair miserable than oors. You lot over there, get some paint and go out and write FUCK THE POPE on every wall you come to. You start a football team to engender a long and bitter history of bigotry and sectarian violence favouring the ruling elite," he cracked his knuckles and opened his codpiece, pulling out his semi-erect penis. "And you, my dear, get yer gums roon' that!"

“When the inappropriately named Defenders attacked Protestant weavers and farmers in Armagh in 1795 the Orange Order which opposes tyranny and despotism in Church and State was re-organised. It is relevant today in a world beset by conflicting systems. In Northern Ireland it faces descendants of the misnamed defenders - Sinn Fein/IRA.

“May these pages help you to understand our position better. May we all discover the Truth which sets us free.”

Mission statement of the web site of the Grand Orange Lodge of Ireland

(http://www.grandorange.org.uk/)

Chapter 1:
QUITE RECENTLY IN NORTHERN IRELAND

There had been a scandal in the papers about the British Army operating a shoot to kill policy in Northern Ireland, like when the SAS topped those cunts in Gibraltar. So now they were operating a shoot to miss policy, which is actually a fuck of a lot harder.

Charley Uncle Norfolk Tango Company had been tracking Ryan O'Brian's crack brigade of Provos for three days. They had reason to believe that they were doing a deal with the Russian Mafia somewhere in the Crossmyarse area close to the border with the Republic; they were getting three SS20s complete with warheads and the Russians were getting three lorryloads of past-its-sell-by-date Spam, some pills that the Provos had stolen in a raid on Boots in East Belfast and nearly three hundred pounds cash that they had saved out of their dole cheques.

The Brits had tracked the Provos down to a lay-by where they had stopped for a fag and to listen to the racing results on the radio. It may have been a cunning ploy, but CUNT Co were taking no chances. They thought about sneaking up on them but thought, ah fuck it. So they just ran at the bastards, screaming and pulling faces and shooting into the air.

"Run like fuck!" shouted Ryan O'Brian, stubbing out his roll-up on the bonnet of their 1969 Capri. "It's the Brits!"

The IRA men scattered, a few grabbed their guns from the back of the car and started shooting back.

"Remember, chaps, aim just above their heads," ordered Lieutenant Carstairs De Vere-Smythington Forbes, who despite the name was actually a grammar school upstart who proved that it wasn't only Old Etonians who made useless and effete officers.

WHAP!
His head burst open sending globby strings of blood and grey brain matter in all directions as an IRA bullet smashed into his gormless face.
"Bugger!" he mumbled as he fell forward into the Old Sod.
"KILL THE KANTS!" ordered Sergeant Nobby 'The Nog' Nobbins, next in the chain of command and not a man to give a toss about what the Guardian had to say. As if to demonstrate what he meant, he shot one of the fleeing IRA soldiers in such a way that the bullet went up his arsehole and out his left nostril via his brain. They train these fuckers good.
Ryan O'Brian had taken on tougher than this, but his team were mostly young and inexperienced and were trying to fire their handguns side on. As a result, young Barney Leary had knocked himself unconscious when his Glock had recoiled and whacked him in the head while wee Terry O'Blimey had accidentally shot three other volunteers.
"WHAT THE HELL ARE YE DOIN' THERE?" he yelled at him. "DID NO CUNT SHOW YOU HOW TO FIRE THAT GUN?"
"That's the way they do it in the fillums!" sobbed O'Blimey.
Ryan O'Brian snatched the gun out of the idiot's shaking hand.
"Run like fuck or I'll shoot you myself!" he snarled.
The remaining Provos ran towards the forest chased by a squad of crazed Brits in camo makeup like they'd seen in Apocalypse Now. Jimmy Deighan, the only other hardened veteran in the squad yelled: "Where the fuck are those Russkies?"

The two gigantic neckless Russians watched the gun battle through binoculars from a few hundred yards away.
Mad Ivan Karamazov, ex KGB and Spetznaz, now an enforcer for the Moscow mob, considered the options:
1) They take out their Mauser hand-cannons and go to the aid of the besieged and outnumbered IRA men.
2) They run like fuck back across the border.
3) They come in on the side of the Brits who are looking like

the winners, just like in Great Patriotic War.
4) They unwrap one of the SS20s and nuke the lot.

"Who we kill?" asked his sidekick Yuri 'The Terrible' Raskolnikov, the biggest serial killer in the history of the USSR, now employed by an organisation where his talents were put to good use.
Mad Ivan shrugged: "Who you fancy?"
"Let's kill British," he said.
"OK!" agreed Mad Ivan.
"With bare hands," said Yuri, throwing down his gun and stripping off his Armani jacket and Yoji Yamamoto shirt with matching watered grey silk Issey Miyake cravat.
"With bare hands," nodded Mad Ivan following his lead.

The surviving IRA men had landed in a foxhole in the woods and were holding off the Brits with blanket covering fire.
The Brits from CUNT Co surrounded them and prepared to wait.
Suddenly the two giant Russians crashed through the woods and began to crack skulls and break necks. The stunned Brits let off a few rounds but they just sank into solid layers of packed fat and muscle without noticeably bothering the two psychotic Russian killers. Yuri The Terrible picked up the a screaming Brit, put him over his knee and snapped his spine.
Mere seconds later only a few of the Brits were still alive, though hopelessly and horribly maimed, and their screams sang out in the woods like the chorus of the damned.
"Top of morning to you," said Mad Ivan to Ryan O'Brian.
"We much like drink your Irish stout," said Yuri. "Though now I settle for blood of British dog."
"Aye," said Ryan O'Brian. "Feel free...erm...have yous brought the bombs we were after?"
"Da," said Mad Ivan. "You come see. You have the money?"
"Aye, back at the car," said Ryan. "C'mon we'll walk back up that way first. Jimmy, youse lot wait here, alright?"

"Right, volunteer O'Brian," agreed Deighan.

They walked back to the Capri and Ryan O'Brian handed them a wad of cash which they inspected thoroughly, rejecting notes that were worn and torn, looking for the magnetic strip. Ryan had to fish a few new tenners out of his wallet to replace some dog eared ones that they didn't want. He gave them the bag of pills and the keys to the van full of meat.
"We'll need the van back, alright?" Said Ryan O'Brian.
"Da," agreed the Russian.
The Russians took Ryan to their van and showed him the three SS20s, wrapped up in newspaper, sitting in the back.
"Is there an instruction book or something?" he asked.
"Nyet," said Mad Ivan. "Is easy to work. Press buttons here, so. Launch then *BOOOOOOMMMMM*!"
"Aye," nodded the Irishman. "Boom boom."
"You are happy with purchase?" asked Yuri.
"Well, as far as it goes, aye," said Ryan O'Brian.
Suddenly the two Russian's heads exploded in a splattering pop of gore and grey matter as a single rocket launched projectile terminated them both with extreme prejudice.
Ryan O'Brian's heart sank as a lardy crew of tattooed Ulster Freedom Fighters led by Billy Boyne surrounded him, pointing their absurd Surface To Air Missile launchers directly at his face.
"Put that thing down, you silly bastard, or you'll blow the friggin' lot of us tae hell!" he snapped.
"Awright, ya Papish cunt!" said Billy Boyne pulling up his ski mask to reveal his miserable porky Prod features. "What's in the back?"
"It's yer mammy, Billy, she's giein line ups for aw' the Bhoys at ten pee a shot," said Ryan O'Brian. "I think she's made a hundred quid by now."
"That's it, just kill the cunt!" he ordered one of his henchmen, a huge blubbery rubber human turd whose Rangers FC strip never quite covered his flaccid white stomach.

The fat bloke started fumbling with the shoulder launched SAM.
"No wi' that, ya fucking eedjit!" said Billy. "Use a fuckin' blade like I tellt ye. D'ye know how much these things cost?"
"Sorry..." mumbled the fat man.
"Look, Billy, you don't know who you're tangling with here," said Ryan O'Brian. "The IRA? That's just a front for me. I'm into something much bigger and you should'nae have yer nose in it. So be a good boy and just piss of back tae yer Shankhill shitehole and we'll say no more about it, OK?"
"Do him!" ordered Billy Boyne.
Ryan O'Brian sighed.
"Beam me up, Scotty," he said rolling his eyes to heaven.

"One of the biggest public relations hoaxes ever perpetrated by the British Crown is that King Edward VIII - who abdicated the throne in 1938 - due to his support for the Nazis, was a "black sheep," an aberration in an otherwise unblemished Windsor line. Nothing could be further from the truth. The British monarchy, and the City of London's leading Crown bankers, enthusiastically backed Hitler and the Nazis, bankrolled the Fuhrer's election, and did everything possible to build the Nazi war machine, for Britain's planned geopolitical war between Germany and Russia.

"Support for Nazi-style genocide has always been at the heart of House of Windsor policy, and long after the abdication of Edward VIII, the Merry Windsors maintained their direct Nazi links.
"So when Prince Philip, co-founder with Prince Bernhard of the Netherlands of the World Wildlife Fund (WWF), tells an interviewer that he hopes to be "reincarnated as a deadly virus" to help solve the "population problem," he is just "doin' what comes naturally" for any scion of the Anglo-Dutch oligarchy...

From: The Nazi Roots of the House of

Windsor
by Scott Thompson
Printed in The American Almanac, August 25, 1997

(http://www.lycos.cs.cmu.edu/wguide/tools/pgview.html?wwbestof=Y&wwtitle=British%20Royal%20Demise&wwdoc=http%3a%2f%2fmembers.tripod.com%2f%7eamerican_almanac%2fnaziroot.htm&wwmid=89709&wwdocid=756661&wwprate=0.50&wwdoctype=2)

CHAPTER 2:

A FEW WEEKS AGO, LONDON AND ROME

Father Pietro tried to stay in the shadows, his head bowed as though in prayer, the cold steel knife concealed beneath his sour-smelling cassock. Rome thronged with priests, nuns, pilgrims and gaudily dressed tourists, gawking at the Chapel Of St Peter and the palace of the Holy Father himself. It was hard to pick out the correct target. But then, just as his superiors in Anus Dei said he would, the whoremaster Masonic collaborator and heretic Father Stephen McTaggart passed, dressed in his slate grey Armani structureless suit (they had been fashionable in the late 1980s but now looked as archaic as the cassock sported by Father Pietro) and clerical collar. He was alone. Father Pietro leaped out of the shadows and with a deft motion of the curved stainless steel kitchen knife, sliced the traitor's throat cleanly open. The Jesuit collapsed and died is a pool of his own steaming blood as the sweating Father Pietro ran back into the shadowy alley.

Grand Master Samuel Wilberforce of the Ancient Order Of Master Masons slammed his fist on the two hundred year old polished oak table. It splintered.
"I am not fucking happy!" he barked to the assembled mafia of the mediocre, seated and dressed in their full regalia. "I am not fucking happy at all. Some cunt has been blabbing his big fucking mouth off. We had a man inside the fucking Vatican itself. Christ, we played our cards right, the cunt could have been the next fucking Pope!"
The elderly English patrician folded his hands behind his back and breathed deeply, trying to calm himself.
"Did they get the cunt wot done it yet?" he hissed.
"The Italian Carbineri arrested a village priest," said ex SAS Commander Andy Shaftesbury, security co-ordinator for the International Zionist Royalist Masonic Conspiracy. "He took a cyanide capsule before he could talk. My informants have tied him Anus Dei, however. To wit, Father Ortega and his Latin mass aficionados."
"Jesus!" spat Wilberforce. "Will these fucking Papist fanatics stop at nothing?"
"It seems that once again you have failed me," said The Queen, pursing her thin dry lips.
All eyes turned to the muscular figure in the twinset who perched on the throne wearing a coronet in which was set the Diadem of the Eastern Star, the secret Masonic crown of English female royalty since 1688.
"Your majesty!" grinned Wilberforce sheepishly. "A mere setback, I promise you."
The Queen sighed.

"It's bad enough having to keep up this facade of being a petite bourgeois constitutional monarch!" she spat. "Without the fraternal brotherhood charged with upholding my true function as an absolute ruler fucking up at every turn! That little Lithuanian prick in Rome must be laughing his blinking socks off!"

Inside the Vatican, Saulus Zdanavich, former Cardinal of Vilnius, Lithuania, now elected to the Throne of St Peter as Pope George Ringo II, smiled and patted the heads of the orphans in his antechamber. Their faces beamed with love and joy at the prospect of meeting the Holy Father himself. Little did they suspect that they were soon going to be carted off to the Vatican's secret medical facility to provide fresh blood to revitalise the Pope and his ailing Cardinals in their forthcoming transfusions.

Father Ryan O'Brian, Belfast IRA Commander and covert religious Jesuit agent, waited impatiently for the Pontiff to finish glad-handing the orphans. He was, without doubt, the dumbest fuck ever to hold the office of Pope. Even dumber than the Polack and that peasant cunt-bag John XXIII with his fucking arse witted Vatican II that had nearly destroyed the church.

"Suffer the little children," he said in flawless Latin.

"Wassat?" barked the Pope, fixing him with his good eye. "You know I don' speak that wop shit so good without a script."

"Nothing your Holiness," he said.

"Please, Father Ryan, call me Saulas. We're all chums here."

"Of course, er, Saulas. Your Holiness."

"Now, to business," the Pope put his arm around Ryan's shoulder. "We got them good today. I'm well impressed. The old bitch must be spitting bile. I'm well chuffed, Ryan, well chuffed."

"You know what I think of the Brits, Your Holiness," he smiled. "It's like old times."

"Now now, Ryan," chided the Pope. "It is still the wish of

mother church to bring the heretic British back into the fold. That has been our fondest hope since that brute Henry went against our wishes and married a whore was back in the 16th century."

"Ah Jaysus, yer Holiness," said Ryan. "You don't surely think that that old bitch is about to come and kiss yer feet, now, do you?"

"No," agreed the Pope. "But I think that her fuckwit of a son might!"

"What is it you're suggesting?"

The Pope smiled and tapped the side of his nose.

"You still got them bombs that you bought from the Russkies?"

"Collusion - a constant factor in the actions of the loyalist death squads

"Sinn Fein North Belfast Assembly representative Gerry Kelly has revealed that following the find of files in an Orange Hall at Stoneyford, an Andersonstown man was visited last evening by the RUC. He was told that his details are in the possession of loyalist death squads and were found in the Orange Hall.

"Mr. Kelly said: 'The man was met by a wall of silence when he tried to find out from the RUC exactly what information the loyalists have.

'I can only assume that the other 299 people identified in these files are now being informed by the RUC that they are on these lists. I would urge anyone approached by the RUC to immediately contact their solicitor and inform Sinn Fein representatives.

‘These files are apparently relatively new and provide hard evidence that collusion has remained a constant factor in the actions of the loyalist death squads. It is further support for the demand for a full public and internationally based inquiry into these matters and especially the Brian Nelson case.

‘In the short term the British Minister with responsibility for the RUC, Adam Ingram, would instruct this force not to withhold vital information from the victims of this conspiracy, information that might save their lives. The RUC should be ordered to provide collusion victims with all of the information on them, which the RUC know to be in the possession of loyalists.’”

Sinn Fein Press Release 5th November 1999

(http://www.sinnfein.ie/)

CHAPTER 3:
ALSO A FEW WEEKS AGO, THE DISGUSTING SLUMS OF GLASGOW

Andy Shaftesbury hated Glasgow with a vengeance, but not as much as he hated Billy Boyne, ex UVF 'berserker', leader-aff of the revitalised Toonheid Billy Boys, major shareholder in Glasgow Rangers PLC and author of the popular monograph *Why Hanging Is Too Good For Tims*. Boyne had never been the same after the ugly incident in Crossmyarse when an entire squad of British troops, six members of an elite IRA squad, two members of what was later discovered to be the Moscow Mafia and a few UDA fuckwits had been found horribly slaughtered with Billy Boyne as the only survivor.
All he could tell his MI5 handlers was that "some Fenian bastard" had "taken" every cunt. It was with a sense of shock that they realised that they were in fact dealing with undercover Jesuit super-agent Father Ryan O'Brian, granted unlimited indulgences by the Pope making him immune to sin and rumoured to have God on his side and to be able to count on divine intervention when he got into sticky situations. Andy didn't really believe that, but still... that was a lot of bodies for one man to leave behind. And HRH wanted some payback.

Billy Boyne, sitting in the King William Of Orange in Govan swilling pint after pint of McEwan's (a former Glasgow Rangers strip sponsor) heavy with his crew, spat as the Reverend Ian Paisley appeared on TV bellowing: "I will not talk to IRA murderers. I will not go to the talks and sit around a table with murderers."
"Fuckin' bastard!" said Billy. "Saft on papacy, the cunt is. Fuckin' traiter tae the Protestant cause."

"Plain to see," agreed Shaftesbury, trying not to gag on the mouthful of sour black vomit-scented liquid that came in pint pots and was referred to as 'heavy'. "The man practically genuflects in the direction of Rome."
"Too fuckin' right!" said Billy. "FTP, ya bas. 1690. Oi oi oi, nae surrender to the IRA!"
The other bluenoses around the table joined in.
"Keep St George in your heart..." began Shaftesbury's sidekick, the forelock-tugging cockernee moron and British National Party sympathiser Sergeant Arfur Brahn (great grandson of the pearly empress made famous in the classic cockernee musical hall song 'Knees Up Muvver Brahn').
Billy pulled out a Stanley knife and held it at Brahn's face. "You just shut it ya English cunt or ah'll slice yer fuckin' coupon open fur ye!"
"Easy," said Shaftesbury. "We're all on the same side here."
"Aye, but youse are fuckin' English," said Billy. "That's no really the same side."
"What, are you fackin SNP or summfink?" Sneered Brahn. "I fort you was Unionists an' not fackin Nationalist IRA scum!"
This had always been a problem for Billy. On one arm he had a tattoo of William III on a white charger. On the other a Lion Rampant with 'Scotland Forever Ya Bas!' He was seemingly unaware or unconcerned about the essential dichotomy of both symbols. If anyone had mentioned it before, he usually responded by chibbing them. They were all for the Union and loyalty to the Queen, but that didn't mean that the fucking English were anything but a bunch of poofs. Look at their churches...there was only a paper wall between the Church Of England and Papal Idolatry. He eyed the Monarchist Masons suspiciously. Didn't the Masons in England take Catholics and Jews now?
"Look," said Shaftesbury. "We like you, Billy. We agree with everything that you stand for. What's the word I'm looking for? that's it - 'mental'. You're 'mental'. In fact you're 'pure mental'. We need a cunt who is 'pure mental', Billy. Are you

'pure mental' enough for us, do you think?"
"Ah'm no just fuckin' mental, pal," said Billy, pulling himself up in his chair, his rancid-bacon complexion turning a deeper pink as he flushed with pride. "Ah'm totally fuckin' pure mental me. See when I was in the UVF? They were gonnae kick me oot for bein' far too fuckin' mental. They had tae make up a special mental squad fur us tae be in. When I kilt a Tim, ah didnae just kill a Tim. Ah kilt his dug, his weans, his mammy, his mammy's mammy. This is nae joken right? Wan time ah hud tae dae this cunt and he hud a budgie. So ah kilt the budgie and rammed it right up the cunt's hole. Just fur a laugh."
The two English military men turned Freemason enforcers smiled uncomfortably at the rancid and pig ignorant lumpen proletarian's tale of unimaginative slaughter.
"The thing is, Billy, we want to pay you a lot of money to do a job for us," said Shaftesbury taking a suitcase of used cash from Brahn and opening it on the table in front of Billy. "£100,000. Would you kill a priest for that Billy?"
Billy smiled.
"Is the Pope a fuckin' Catholic?" he laughed.

CHAPTER 4:

AN INTERLUDE. FLASHBACK: THE VATICAN, 1938

The Pope and his top cardinals were legless on a combination of fortified communion wine and laudanum which special Vatican chemists produced to ease the burdens of God's shepherds. The Orgy Room in the Crypt Of St Peter's Chapel resembled something from a Fullini or Passolini version of the last days of the Roman Empire. Frightened Romanian, Croatian and Irish foundlings and orphans were herded in for the delectation of the cunt-faced clerics.
"Ooh, look at that one," hissed Fr. O'Loughlan, the portly Bishop Of Philadelphia, (a virulent Nazi apologist who was visiting Rome for the first time). "An ass like a goddamn li'l under-ripe peach!"
The altogether more sophisticated European clerics rolled their eyes at the gauchness of the North American. What could one expect from a nation that lad lacked true kingship tied to the magnificence of Rome itself? Still, one had to be tolerant...
"Hey there, boy," the toilet-mouthed Yank leered at the blonde 10 year old. "Why don't y'all just drop your pants and come on over here and park that cute heiney on mah big stiff rod and' staff?"
Liberated from the need to conceal his predilection for pre-teen boys, no longer confined to merely fondling choir boys and wanking off in confessionals, the Bishop was nearly insane with lust.
Stefan, the 10 year old orphan child - taken from his home village in the wilds of Romania with the promise that he would be taken to a good and loving home in the West - had watched in horror as the children were divided into two groups. Those who would go to act as living blood banks, providing transfusions for the decrepit octogenarian Prelates of Rome

and those who were to be used as sex toys in their sickening orgies.

For days he had been poked and abused by various high ranking priests and Vatican dignitaries. He wanted to vomit every time he saw one of them. He hated them now. He swore an oath of vengeance on the church, the Virgin Mary and Christ Jesus and the Saints.

His father had been killed before he was born by a local warlord and his mother had died of starvation when he was six. Stefan had grown up as a feral child, scavenging for food in the village and in the hills around his home. He knew how to take care of himself.

Nicole, Stefan's friend, and Usmilla, his sister, were taken away to be drained and eaten.

"They will serve the Holy Fathers in their most exquisite Communion," said the Jesuit slaver who was in charge of the eight or nine who remained. "You, my little pretties, will serve in other ways."

Stefan, who knew some Latin, listened and learned as various priests came to inspect them. They were fed and washed and dressed in new clothes that did not crawl with lice.

And then a drunken monk took Stefan aside. He was a Romanian and had managed to sneak into a forbidden part of the Vatican.

"Listen, young one, I know you're too young to understand," he said. "I was once used as you will be and now I am a slave here in Rome. But I have discovered terrible things. You must try and escape...all of you. There is a vent behind the Papal throne. You must get all the children to safety, out of here...you must run, child Go to the catacombs...there are others there like you."

Just then the Jesuit slaver arrived accompanied by Thompson sub-machine gun sporting Swiss Guards who seized the monk.

"Remember...It is all a lie!" he screamed as they dragged him away. "All of it...*UKK!*"

Then the Jesuit returned with two Cardinals dressed in purple

robes and dripping in jewels. They looked like old women, their pale lascivious faces painted and rouged.
They talked in excited, high-pitched voices about what they wanted to do to the children. Stefan alone understood...

He smiled and went over to the quaking American, seemingly oblivious to the cries of distress from the other children as leering Cardinals and Bishops groped and prodded them, breathing boozy halitosis-scented breath in their innocent faces.
Stefan looked around quickly and, with two deft movements of his thumbs, gouged out the cardinal's eyes and then snapped his windpipe with a single blow before he could utter a scream. It took a few seconds before the other priests noticed and began screaming. Stefan motioned for the other children to follow him and then they ran. The Pope, aware of what was happening but too wasted to care, pressed the red button to summon the guards. The children scattered, through legs and under cassocks, swiftly ducking and veering away from the fumbling Vicars of Christ who attempted to grab them. One sweating and lumbering Sicilian peasant priest attempted to stand in their way. Stefan picked up a heavy cut crystal dish laden with stuffed larks and smashed it as hard as he could up the priest's cassock, cleaving the fascist fucker's turgid todger in clean in half.
The fat priest howled and fell over bleeding to death. The Swiss Guards stormed in.
"Shoot them!" slurred the hawk faced Pope.
Fortunately, in the late '30s, firearms were still notoriously poorly made, difficult to aim and prone to jams and misfires. The Swiss Guard opened up their Thomson sub-machine guns, aiming at the children, but only succeeding in splattering the room with the fat and guts of more priests. The children ducked through an air conditioning vent, Stefan standing guard until the last one was through before escaping himself.
"They're getting away, you cunts!" barked the Pope, who had

now sobered up. "After them!"
But the Swiss Guards could not get into the vent. The Pope stumbled over and started kicking their bottoms.
"Idiots!"

Stefan led the children through the walls of the Vatican and into the catacombs beneath. When he judged that it was safe, they rested amidst the mummified corpses of the martyrs and ancient Roman saints in the endless tunnels beneath the seven hills. Stefan did not know where they were. Perhaps they had fallen into Hell. Well, better this Hell than their Heaven, he thought. They would stay here and grow strong and when the time was right...the Pope and all his minions had better beware!

"To get beyond the soap opera stuff and truly understand the Windsors today, it is useful to start with Prince Philip. Not only was he trained in the Hitler Youth curriculum, but his German brothers-in-law, with whom he lived, all became high-ranking figures in the Nazi Party.

"Before his family was forced into exile, Prince Philip had been in line of succession to the Greek throne, established after a British-run coup against the son of King Ludwig of Bavaria, who became King Otto I of the Hellenes. Having dispatched King Otto in 1862, London ran a talent search for a successor, which resulted in the selection of Prince William, the son of the designated heir and nephew to the Danish king, Crown Prince Christian. In 1862, Prince William of the Danes was installed as King George I of Greece, and married a granddaughter of Czar Nicholas I in 1866. Prince Philip is a grandson of Queen Victoria, and he is related to most of the current and former crowned heads of Europe, including seven czars.

"Through the influence of his sister Theodora, young Philip was sent to the German school near Lake Constantine that had been founded by Berthold's father, Max von Baden, working through his longtime personal secretary, Kurt Hahn. During World War I, Prince Max von Baden had been chancellor, while the Oxford-trained Hahn first served as head of the Berlin Foreign Ministry's intelligence desk, then as special adviser to Prince Max in the Versailles Treaty negotiations. Von Baden and Hahn set up a school in a wing of Schloss Salem, employing a combination of monasticism and the Nazis' "strength-through-joy" system. At first a supporter of the Nazis, Hahn, who was part Jewish, soon got into trouble with the SS, and came to support the more centrist elements of the Nazi Party. What Hahn really had become is what Henry Kissinger's friend, Michael Ledeen has termed a "universal fascist", in the sense of Vladimir Jabotinsky, Count Coudenhove-Kalergi, the Strasser brothers, and other fascists whom the hard-core Nazis would have no dealings with.

"Although Hahn's powerful connections permitted him to escape the concentration camps, he was forced to leave the school he founded in Germany before Philip's arrival there, and established a new school in Scotland, called Gordonstoun. It would play a major role in rearing all the male children of Queen Elizabeth II and Philip. When Philip

arrived at Hahn's school in Schloss Salem, it was in control of the Hitler Youth and the Nazi Party, and the curriculum had become Nazi "race science". Hahn became an adviser to the Foreign Office in London, urging policies of appeasement based upon appeals to the "centrist" Nazis."

From *The Nazi Roots Of The House Of Windsor*
by Scott Thompson
Printed in The American Almanac, August 25, 1997.
(http://members.tripod.com/~american_almanac/naziroot.htm)

CHAPTER 5:

RECENTLY, THE GUILD HALL, LONDON

The Queen's husband fought to control a spasm of the Tourette's Syndrome which even the strongest drugs could not suppress. As HRH shook hands with the assembled Commonwealth Heads of State, he followed at a discreet distance, aching to give the gathering of grinning curry-breathed wogs of every hue, chinks, nig nogs and jumped up rat-chewing Third World dictators in their silly uniforms from that ghastly shop on Wigmore Street (all solid gold epaulettes and scrambled eggs on the brows of their caps like one of those nouveau riche tarts the current PM kept introducing to HRH and hubby) a piece of his seething racist mind. Cunts. Ungrateful cunts. He didn't know where half the bloody countries were, particularly the African ones. They all had pretty decent names at one time. British West Africa, British Central Africa. Now it was all bloody unpronounceable - Oogi-Moogliland or some name with no vowels in it, like a Czech goalkeeper.

Shit. He bit his tongue. Had he actually barked like a dog at one of the President-For-Life of bloody Tongo's wives? Maybe not, maybe not.

He would be OK as long as none of the woggoes tried to speak to him.

"Jolly nice to meet you," said some darky in a bloody psychedelic dress, shaking his hand, speaking in a cut glass Home Counties accent. "I trust that you are well?"

He smiled and leaned forward: "I've got my eye on you, Sambo, so just keep your hands to yourself. There's a good boy."

Shit shit shit. Had he actually said that? Or did he in fact say: "Weren't you in the year below me at Gordonstoun?"

There actually was a jiggaboo in the year below him and it could feasibly have been this fellow - though God alone knew how you were supposed to tell them apart.

"How nice of you to remember," the grinning old coon replied. Was he just being polite? Probably not. Politeness was never big among our Commonwealth brethren.

Some wog bint with big tits was talking to HRH. Was it the President of India of some such? Did they still have India or was it all broken up into so-called independent republics? One never knew these days. He knew that India still had a cricket team and all, but that didn't mean much in geopolitical terms. He wedged his hands behind his back to prevent him from giving her tits a good hard squeeze on the way past. That sort of thing never went down well with the plebs in the FO, or The Sun or, most importantly, HRH herself. Always going on about how bloody important it was to keep up appearances.

"Did you ever work in old Madame Fat-Arse's Nameless Bordello on Piccadilly?" he asked as the woman passed.

HRH shot him a dagger.
Bugger. So he had said that one out loud. Still, she did look familiar enough and you can't really put anything past the wogs. I mean, if you're going to have a woman prime minister you might as well have one who's put in a few years on her back sticking away a few quid for a rainy day. Makes them less likely to need a bribe from time to time.

They went in to dinner and HRH gave them the usual spiel...blah blah blah...working together as equals (hah!)...fraternity of nations....all democratic now...Christ alone knew why they kept up this charade!
The waiters were under strict instructions not to give him any booze, so while the rest of the delegates got merrily rat-arsed, he sat there sipping near-beer and playing with his food while some boring little arsehole from an emergent nation went on about the problems of the water-table and the starvation and the lack of bloody investment and the debt to the banks and the AIDS crisis...
Eventually he couldn't take it any more.
"Look here, Rastus or whatever the hell your name is," he hissed. "All of your bloody problems come down to the fact that you can't control the old one eyed trouser snakes. There are just too many of you. Here's a hint: keep your peckers in your pants - as we used to say in the Navy - and your bints won't go dropping picanninies all over the shop and you won't have lots of nancy boys popping off and taking up all the hospital space. Ergo there'll be more chow to go around and your bank manager might not feel so bloody scared to advance you a few shekels every once in a while."
The democratically elected African president stared at him dumbfounded.
The Duke winced. Another telling off from HRH and another humiliating apology was on the cards.

CHAPTER 6

DOMESTIC COLLECTION DIVISION

Foreign Intelligence Information Report
Directorate of Intelligence

WARNING NOTICE - INTELLIGENCE SOURCES AND METHODS INVOLVED FURTHER DISSEMINATION AND USE OF THE INFORMATION SUBJECT TO CONTROLS STATED AT BEGINNING AND END OF REPORT

REPORT CLASS: TOP SECRET REPORT NO: 00.D 831/173466-97
COUNTRY: France
DATE DISTR: 17 June 1997
SUBJECT: File overview: Diana Princess Of Wales-Dodi
REFERENCES DCI Case 64376
SOURCE: CASParis/CASLondon/COSGeneva/CASKingston/UK citizen Ken Etheridge

1. Relationship initiated between Diana POW and Dodi aF according to reliable intel sources in November 1996. Intimacy begins shortly after they meet. (Report filed)

2. Reliable source reports Palace seriously disturbed by liaison. PM considers any al Fayed relationship politically disastrous. Edinburgh (Prince Philip -ed) sees serious threat to dynasty should relationship endure. Quote reported: "Such an affair is racially and morally repugnant and no son of a Bedouin camel trader is fit for the mother of a future king," Edinburgh. (Report filed)
3. Request from highest circles to DEA attaché UK for 6 on Dodi re: Cocaine. See File forwarded to UK embassy DC. (Copy filed)

4. US liaison to MI6 requested by David Spedding for assistance in providing permanent solution to Dodi problem. Blessing of Palace secured (Twiz filed)

5. WHuse (White House -ed) denies Spedding request. Harrison authorized only to arrange meeting for MI6 representative with K-Team Geneva. (Twiz on file)

6. Meeting in Geneva reportedly successful (Report filed)

7. al Fayed Mercedes Limo stolen and returned with electronics missing. Reliable

intel source confirms K-team involved. Source reports car rebuilt to respond to external radio controls. (Report filed)

8. COBGeneva reports that on May 28, 1997 heavily weighted Fiat Turbo . . . . (end of page text)

Purported CIA Report on the 'Murder' of Princess Diana (http://209.204.197.55/dodi-1.html)

Father Ryan O'Brian was ushered into the hunting lodge by an embarrassed looking courtier to meet three English aristocrats dressed in absurd shooting clothes that, frankly, stank to buggery. The heir to the British throne, a balding jug-eared chinless inbred in an absurd flat cap, advanced to the priest and kissed his ring.

"Is this correct? Should one bow?" he asked, slightly embarrassed.

"You're the heir to the fucking throne and the Church Of fucking England, you thick cunt," spat his younger more robust brother. "Of course you don't fucking bow."

As if to underline the point, he gripped the ex-IRA man's hand and shook it vigorously.

"How do you do," he said sternly. "I hear you were in the IRA? Did you kill my uncle?"

"Not personally," smiled the priest. "Though I know a man who did."

"Look here," squeaked the prince who was the youngest and reputedly most useless of the three royals. "Can we get on with this?"

"Shut it, puff!" the other two princes said in unison.
"Well, boys," grinned Father Ryan O'Brian. "Getting down to business might not be such a bad idea. His Holiness has asked me to convey to you his wishes to end this senseless conflict and arrive at an amicable accord. After all, the Yids and the Arabs are running amok and it seems to me - and His Holiness of course - that it's ludicrous for Christendom's finest to be fighting a long running and costly covert war amongst ourselves."
"Yes," agreed the jug-eared prince. "Though with many of our subjects of the Hebrew faith as well as the Islamic, Hindu and indeed, a whole rainbow of beliefs..."
"Cut the crap," said the Irish Priest. "You don't have any subjects. You're just waiting in the wings getting older and older. The bitches in your family live a long time, I'm told."
"Granny's 1000 this year!" squealed the youngest Prince.
"Shut it puff!" the other two said in unison.
"What I'm saying is that you could be drawing your pension yourself before she cops. Am I right?" smiled Ryan O'Brian.
The heir to the throne nodded sheepishly.
"The thing is..." began the middle brother.
"We want you to kill mummy for us," said the youngest. "We'll pay you oodles of money and be nice to His Holiness. We'll give the Falklands to the Argentinians and let Ireland kick all the Prods out. You can even have Gibraltar back if you like."
"Shut it, puff!" said the other two princes in unison.
"Now now," said Father Ryan O'Brian. "Surely nice boys like you don't want to go killing your mummy? That's a bad sin. The baby Jayus would be very upset."
"It's her or me," stammered the heir to the throne. "She's upset. She had my ex-wife done in. She said it was for the good of the state. It's not my fault that her boyfriend was, um, of the Muslim persuasion. Mummy blamed me, you see. She wouldn't let me marry the woman I loved, so I hitched up with this silly girl. Mummy now says that she was nothing but a common trollop. It wasn't my fault that she went and shacked

up with some Arab fellow..."
"And she was going to tell the papers that his Mr Squirty Sausage was out of order," chuckled the middle brother, poking the heir to the throne in the groin.
"So she's making me sign a deal that cuts me out of being King in favour of my youngest boy," said the prince, sadly.
"Except we're not really sure that he is yours anymore, are we Mr Floppy Slug?" said the youngest prince.
"Shut it puff," the other two said in unison.
Ryan O'Brian smiled. If people knew how lame these chinless cunts really were, they'd rise up and hang them from lamp-posts in minutes. These effete clods were perfect.
"Well now, lads, I think we can do some business here..."

"""I learned much from the Order of the Jesuits. Until now there has never been anything more grandiose on the earth than

the hierarchal organisation of the Catholic Church. I transferred much of this orgnisation into my party...I am going to let you in on a secret...I am founding an order...In my "Burgs" of the Order, we will raise up a youth which will make the world tremble"...Hitler then stopped, saying that he couldn't say any more..."

Hitler M'a Dit **by Hermann Rauschning**

CHAPTER 7

Publicly avuncular, the self styled Sheikh Hassan I Sabbah Abdul Al Hazred, owner of the sprawling and ancient Herods department store, a toady to the British establishment who was cruelly spurned by the same, surveyed the guests at his swinging Christmas party who were getting progressively drunker on his champagne, stuffed on his food and blasted out of their tiny little fucking minds on his 100% pure cocaine.

Popular disc jockey Fat Seb Tongue was spinning his hot dance tunes while the assembled debutante totty and their chin-deficient escorts danced stiffly while salivating paparazzi buzzed around like ravenous bluebottles, pricks erect at the thought of the lucrative fees that they would pick up from OK, Hello and Tits Out magazines for these shots.

The horse faced, big-titted socialite Lady Arabella Wonkington-Smythe and her friend the Hon Ffyyiaunnaugh Tomkinson Bonkinson danced daintily around their Prada handbags and simulated oral sex with each other as the besotted photographers alternated between pulling themselves off and firing off the shots that would grace tomorrow's Sun, along with the headline: **POSH LEZZIES GET TITS OUT FOR SUN - EXCLUSIVE!** Meanwhile a few chinless newspaper columnists and their ugly bluestocking opposite numbers mentally composed their week's columns around this pseudo event: Is Lesbianism The New Rock And Roll? and Do Gels Become Lezzies Because Chaps Are Naff In Bed? (Honk!).

The fat sheikh cracked open a vial of amyl-nitrate, pausing to shake hands with mullet-haired chum Pepe Ropeman, owner of the celebrated upper class nite spot and lap dancing bar Bimbos, and fat film director Michael Loser (who looked like Jabba The Hut's arsehole had sprouted legs).

He'd show them all. Every last one of those pale faced, toothless, effete, sneering bastards. He had pulled himself up by his bootstraps from the slums of Syria and had built a thriving business empire in London based around Herods, the top people's department store. Then, his son Ali, had become the escort of the Princess Of Wales, the Goddess incarnate on Earth, the most beloved woman in the world. It was a dream come true for Hassan. Soon they would have to accept him. No more sneering at him for wearing the wrong shoes to the hunt.

But fate dealt him a cruel blow. Acting on orders from the evil husband of the Queen, Freemason agents of the dreaded English Intelligence Death Squad led by their dastardly chief M had assassinated both of them to spare their lilly-white English throne from the stain of a brown Arab baby...

Burning with hate and a desire for revenge, he bided his time. Soon, he thought, he would have the Queen grovelling before him after fighting a duel of honour with her husband, the man responsible for the murder of his son...Then, in the classic gangster tradition, he would take the Queen as his own bitch, crowning himself King Hassan I The First, King-Emperer Of

The Unholy British Empire!.

Lost in this reverie, he barely noticed the Roman Catholic priest standing beside him. The priest smiled. Hassan smiled back. He distrusted them, the Catholics. They had launched their crusades against his people 900 odd years ago and it wasn't until they got their arses kicked at Acre that they had been forced to withdraw. Now with their bastard Jew fronted fortress state they had re-established a foothold there. Still...anyone who also had a grudge against the Crown...my enemy's enemy and all that...

"Nice party," said the Priest.
"Thank you father....?"
"Father Ryan O'Brian, SDI," the cheerful Irish priest gripped him warmly by the hand. "Special Envoy of His Holiness the Pope."
"The Pope? In Rome?"
"None other," smiled the Irishman. "Oh, the Pope has heard all about you, sir. He was most disappointed not to be allowed to come here on a shopping trip when he visited London a few years ago. They had him off ministering to sick kids in the East End or something, but he said that there's nothing he'd rather have done than visit Herods for a wee spot of shopping. A look around the food hall, maybe a wee something from the world famous Aztec Room..."
"Really?"
"Oh, aye. Y'know, His Holiness was only saying to me the other day. 'Ryan' he says 'It's a pity yon fella isn't a Catholic. Not that I've anything against the Moslems you understand, but a fella like that could be a big asset to the church'. Oh aye, you could be a big man if you were in with the Mother Church."
"What, *really!?*"
"But I says to him I says 'Well, it's like this yer Holiness. The fella's well in there with the English royal family an' all.

They're going to give him a passport and make him a Knight and give him his own chair at the House Of Lords an' everything' I says 'So the fella wouldn't be interested in something like...Oh, I don't know....getting made a Bishop or one of those medals you're always givin' out to those fellas in the funny hats or a job with the Knights Of Gibraltar'"
"The Knights Of Gibraltar?"
"Och, a grand bunch of lads," smiled the Jesuit. "Bankers, businessmen, politicians, a bit like yourself. They get together and dress up once a year and get a lot of titles and do some work for charity and all and every so often His Holiness blesses them. They get to go to Heaven without any time in Purgatory and if they should ever commit a sin, say murder or the like, it gets forgiven right away."
"It's a pity that I don't hold to your faith, father," smiled the avuncular, revenge-driven, portly and slightly mad Arab.
"Ah, who does, sir," said the Priest. "It's only a bit of a laugh, really. Still, I'll go back to Rome and tell His Holiness that you said thanks but no thanks."
"Wait, wait," smiled the sweating store keeper. "That wasn't exactly what I was saying...I think I'd be interested in working with the Pope...after all, we all have, er, problems in common that need, ah, *solving*..."
"That we do, sir, that we do". The Priest looked around the store. "You know, it was a bit before your time here. But I planted a bomb just over there, oh, a few years ago now. Funny to be back here now..."

CHAPTER 8

THE TINY LATIN AMERICAN NATION OF SAN CHRISTOPHER, (A THINLY

DISGUISED FICTIONAL COLOMBIA).

Father Gonzales said the last rites over the bullet splattered body of Abel Rodriguez, Marxist guerrilla and freedom fighter who'd been killed following a two hour gun battle in which the cornered Red Hero had singlehandedly slaughtered over 50 amazingly incompetent members of the fascist military police death squads of the Neo-Peronist Generalissmo Jesus Montoya.

In the street outside the surviving jackbooted cops, guns still reeking of cordite, rounded up and raped, tortured and murdered innocent civilians at random and began hauling the corpses off their comrades off the streets. Father Gonzales, his faith tried to breaking point by the atrocities that he daily witnessed, looked into his heart and asked whose side Christ would have been on. More and more, he concluded, Christ would have been fighting alongside the guerrillas in the hills around the capital of Cortez City.

Over the next few weeks, as he tried to comfort his parishioners - the poor, the dispossessed and the homeless children of the city - Father Gonzales arrived at a Marxist interpretation of history and saw that the only course of action compatible with his conscience was to support revolutionary action by and of the people. A broad alliance of peasants, Indians, workers, intellectuals, students, soldiers and petite bourgeois elements, he reasoned, must overthrow the ruling US backed plutocracy cum narco-Nazi regime, nationalise the country's assets and plough the profits from the lucrative cocaine trade back into social programs.

And more and more he came to realise that the Church had historically sided with the oppressors and was perverting the true message of Christ which was, when all was said and done, a message of radical love and revolutionary action.

Father Gonzales stashed his well thumbed copy of Das Kapital back in its secret hiding place, dressed in the simple homespun rag-cassock and walked back towards the church on the corner of the street. The rude shack was surrounded by tents where homeless families congregated for spiritual comfort and for the free food, education, medical aid programs and Marxist day schools that Father Gonzales had started - and, of course, to use the building for clandestine meetings where they discussed how best to give support to the communist freedom fighters hiding in the hills.

A few of the poor folk shook his hand - he discouraged ring kissing and other displays of abasement - and clapped him on the back. Then he heard a voice.

"Father Gonzales?"
He turned to see two Priests, dressed in black suits, wearing wide brimmed hats and RayBan glasses.
"Yes, I am he," said the Priest.
One of the Priests In Black produced a badge in a wallet and flashed it: Father Gonzales froze with terror.
"Holy Office," said the stranger, coldly. "You will come with us please."
Father Gonzales threw up his hands and laughed despite his fear .
Whilst a Rhodes scholar at Oxford he'd become a massive fan of the surrealist English comedy programme, Monty Python's Flying Circus.
"Nobody expects the Spanish Inquisition! Cardinal Fang, the comfy pillow!"he yelled while reaching around for his concealed .38.
The startled Inquisitors broke left and right, reaching for their own weapons. *KRAK!* Gonzales caught one of them in the thigh with a lucky shot. The pig screamed. His concealed

colleague returned fire, *KRAK! KRAK! KRAK! KRAK!* The fascist's back up goon squad - members of the elite Jesuit trained Torquemada Battalion of the Vatican's Latin American Counter Insurgency Police SWAT Squad - came crashing in, bayonet tipped M16's at the ready.
Father Gonzales never had a chance. The hail of hot lead ripped his body to to bloody shreds. He collapsed to his knees, and, while coughing blood and praying to Jesus for help, fired of one last wild shot which ricocheted of the crude hard-wood crucifix above the altar and hit the commanding officer smack between the eyes. The Police captain, holding an M16 on full automatic in each hand, whirled in a complete circle, his trigger fingers tightening, spraying the room with metal-jacketed pain and trauma in his spastic death throes. His highly trained body of combat-coke stoked crack fascist super-cops squealed like really soft pigs with embarrassingly low pain-thresholds as a surprisingly large number of the illegal dum-dum bullets (each one designed to tear a dinner-plate sized chunk of flesh out the human body) seemed uncannily prone to zero in on the few vulnerable chinks in their bullet proof Kevlar all-over body-armour. And then an especially freakish shot hit a white phosphorous grenade which exploded, spraying its deadly contents in all directions.
"*Aaaargh! Fuck! Oh no! My Legs! My eyes! Mother! Mother, please! My eyes are burning! Please, for pity's sake, please shoot meeeeeeee! Aaaaaargh! Shut up you soft cunt, look at me, I've just had both my fucking arms blown off! AAARGH! And both cunting legs! SHIT! OH, MAN! NOT MY FUCKING BALLS, MAN! AAAAAAARGH! PLEASE KIIIIIIILL MEEEEEEE!*" screamed the narco-nazi cops in Spanish as more high explosive and WP grenades exploded in a savage, miraculously unlikely and utterly lethal chain reaction which sprayed expensively trained fascist pig body parts in all directions.
"That's another 64 of the bastards dead!" chuckled Father Gonzales as he sprawled on his back in a slowly spreading

pool of his own blood and surveyed the unbelievable carnage. Slowly he raised his right fist in salute to the bullet pock-marked crucifix above the altar. He wheezed and coughed his way through the first two verses of the Spanish language version of The Internationale. And then he died.
Another innocent victim of the frothgobbed, swivel eyed and gibberingly insane global death struggle between two utterly evil empires. Oh when would the madness end?

"But pause to think. Better still, feel the back of your own neck - four, five inches in length? A small target indeed for the man standing over you, his knuckles white as he grips the axe, his nerves taut and twitching under the concentrated gaze of thousands of spectators. Will he sway off aim as you stare

blindly down into the waiting basket? If he does, will you instinctively bring your hands up, only to have them amputated by his second strike?"

Lords Of The Scaffold **by Geoffrey Abbott**

CHAPTER 9

The Queen strained away on her private lavatory in the legendary Baked Bean room - an annex of Buckingham palace that visitors were never shown. The room was, of course, an urban myth. It was also a sad and rather sordid reality.

The Baked Bean Room was where members of the Royal Family, seeking release from their arsegrindingly oppressive chore of meeting and greeting "the scum", could give vent to their wildest and most disgusting fantasies in total privacy.

Think about it. Visiting shit-holes like Leeds or Coventry. Having to ask polite questions of grovelling mongrels, half-breeds, half-wits, crippos, work-shy morons, sexual degeneratres and thick-as-fuck peasants with pig shit under their stubby little fingernails. Having to smile like a wanking dolphin for hours and fucking hours on end. Having to shake hands with hundreds of fish'n'chip reeking gutter filth wearing nasty plastic clothes. Having to appear interested in their tedious, dull little bourgeois lives. Never being able to say "And so what do your do? Like I give a fuck, you noisome little un-bred fucking nonentity!" Having to accept endless bouquets of flowers from cute little girls while all the time fighting back the almost irresistible urge to bend down, rip the little fucker's head off and then suck the blood from the cunt's spurting neck

stump. And - worst of all - *never being able to fart!*
And that *was* the worst part of it, thought the Queen, letting out a 240 decibel 4.9 on the Richter scale sphincter-ripper with a huge grunt.
Hence the Baked Bean Room.

The room's dominant feature was, of course, a huge trough of baked beans which were pumped in daily via an underground pipe line from a secret factory in the English midlands.
There was nothing the Queen liked more, after a hard day on her best behaviour amongst the great unwashed, than stripping off bollock naked and swimming in the vast lake of beans, wolfing them down feverishly, farting like a mad dog and screaming "*FUUUUUUUUUCK*!" and "*CUUUUUUUUUUNT*!" and "*DIE YOU BLACK BAAAAAAAAAAAAAAAAAAAARSTARDS*!" and suchlike at the top of her voice. It came as such a relief!

"Come on out you fucking CUNT!" roared the Queen as she nursed a stubborn turtle's head out of her partially dilated anus with her left index finger, letting rip an ear-shattering fart as she did so.
"*Jesus FUUUUUUUUUK!*" she screamed as she tried to void her royal bowels of the rather stodgy fare on which she had dined with the American President and his frankly rather ghastly wife the night before. The USA was still a vassal state of the English monarchy, despite the fiction of 1776, and traditionally the American President had to present the English monarch with the deep-fried hearts of 200 new born infants every year to ensure her good graces.
Well tradition be dammed! - thought HRH - next year we'll change it to something a little more bloody digestible!
"Uh uh uh uh uh UUUUUUUUUUUUUH! (plop) *Aaaaaaaaaaaaaaaah*!"
Leaning back, the Queen sparked up an opium fag and relaxed like a boneless dog.

Fuck it! - thought the Queen (who was so well bred that she seldom if ever even *thought* a swear word outside the confines of the Baked Bean room) - today's my fun day, my I-don't-have-to-fucking-run-day! Time to chill, motherfucker!
And so, picking up a plastic backed copy of her favourite book, *Raiders Of The Low Forehead* by Stanley Manly, she settled down for good read while she waited for the next inevitable wave of crippling and mind-bogglingly excruciating stomach cramps. She was soon belly laughing, tears cutting paths through the congealed baked bean sauce on her cheeks, as she once again revelled in the hilarious antics of the thick Northern scummoes.
Raiders was of course published by Attack! Books and the Queen was a massive fan of all the avant-pulp outfit's output. There were a stack of books on the floor - *Tits-Out Teenage Terror Totty* by Steven Wells, *Satan! Satan! Satan!* by Tony White, *Get Your Cock Out* by Mark Manning and, of course, *Whips and Furs: My Life as a Bon Vivant, Gambler and Love Rat* by Jesus H. Christ (introduced and abridged by Stewart Home).
"Hmmm. what's this?" murmured HRH as she came to the end of *Raiders*. It was a shamelessly opportunistic advert for three new Attack! books - *Bloody Heroes* by Bob Morris, *Ebola 3000* by Richard Marshall and - oh joy! - *Tokyo Bloodbath 2002* by her favourite author, Stanley Manly! Brilliant! She made a mental note to get an equerry to send a cheque for the special discount price of £18.00 for all three books off to *Attack! c/o Creation Books, 4th Floor, City House, 72-80 Leather Lane, London EC1N 7TR* today. It was the same address she'd sent £9.99 to for her Attack! Club membership - the certificate for which was hanging framed on the wall in front of her.
"This is to certify that HRH The Queen is Attack! Club member 0000000000000000000015 and is therefore a good bloke - OFFICIAL!"
She still remembered the thrill she got when she opened up the

package that she got back from Attack! and had pulled out the superbly printed "In your face, down your trousers and up your arse like a shit eating rabbit on speed!" Attack! T-shirt which, of course, was all she ever wore around the Baked Bean Room. Apart from really pervy sex-gear and a schnorkel, obviously.
"*PRAAAAAAAAAAAAAAAAAAAAAAAAAARP*!" exploded the Queen's arse savagely.
Here we go again!
"*Pppppparp!* Uh! *Quack!* Uh uh! Uh! *Parp!* Uh uh uh! *FiiiiiiiiiiiizPARP!* Uh uh! UH! COME ON YOU *BASTARD*! *PARP!* Uh! *QUACK*! Just....one.....more....*push*! Uh! *PAAAAAAAAAAAAAAAAAAAAAAAAAAAAAAARa AAAAAAAAAAAAAAAAAAAAAAAP!* UH! Splash! Plop! *Siiiiiiiiiiiiiiiiiiiiiiiiiiiiiiiiiiiiiiiiiiiiiiiiiiiiiiiiiiiiigh!*"

The Queen fumbled for another drug-fag, sparked up and wiped her royal arse with luxurious 4-ply toilet paper imprinted with the scowling features of the current Pope. She had once employed an especially trained squad of blind, lobotomised orphans to carry out this chore for her but the Queen Mother, in the throes of one of her regular cannibalistic binge-frenzies, had eaten them all on Boxing Day, 1998.
"Jesus fucking Christ being shafted up the arse by a blind nun equipped with a steel-studded dildo! I needed that!" she grunted, letting out one last earth-shatteringly violent fart before pulling the chain and preparing to toss herself straight back into the slimy baked bean depths.

"Your majesty," coughed the blind equerry stood in the corner of the room. "Might I respectfully remind you, ma'am, that you'll be shitting in the Prime Minister's face in 12 minutes?"

The Queen groaned. By tradition she defecated onto the face of the Prime Minister once a week, the politician then loyally licking her anus and arse-cheeks clean as a sign of his dehumanised subservience. The current Tory PM, however, seemed to enjoy the ritual rather more than he really should.

"Yes! Yes!" snapped the Queen, irritably. "One more dip in the beans and I'll be ready. Tell my maid to lay out the green dress, the one with the flowers on. And the arseless knickers, obviously."

She dismissed him, went to the window and stared down at the crowds of over-awed tourists and thicko forelock-tugging Brits that were always milling around outside Buckingham Palace.

Ordinary people, she thought. What cunts.

SHLOP! What was that!? The Queen whirled. And stared straight into the gaping muzzles of an Uzi 9mm machine-pistol (600 rounds per minute, effective range 100 meters) and a 32oz 9mm Browning Hi-Power automatic pistol (with a 13 round clip). The guns were being held in the hands of a muscular frogman who was emerging slowly, like the Lady of The Lake (except accompanied by a hideous slurping sound) from the vast pool of baked beans.

"Shit!" barked the Queen. This could only mean that the Vatican had infiltrated the secret baked bean pipeline. And that could only mean one thing - *that there was a traitor in the House Of Windsor!*

"Guards!" she yipped.
"Save your breff, you stack ap cah!" snarled the frogman, "No facker'll hea...Jeezuz Fack! It fackin pen and fackin inks in 'ere! Fack me! Have you got bowel cancer or sumfink? Jeezus fackin' wept!"
The Queen smiled as she heard the coarse cockernee accent. At least now she knew she had a chance!
"Give your guns to me and prepare to die!" she commanded.
"Oh yeah!" laughed the rubber-clad cockernee assassin."You

mast fink oim fackin fick or sumfink, knowarramean?"
But, much to his surprise, he found himself handing over his weapons, which were then pointed at his face.
"What the fack!?" gasped the confused cockernee frogman.
"Wot I go an' fackin' do that for? Eh!"
"It's because you're a cockernee" smiled the Queen, enjoying the feel of the superbly weighted guns in her well-trained hands. "Of all the groups of forelock -tugging plebeian scum it is my duty to rule over" she continued, "you cockernees have always been the most servile and stupid. It's not your fault, it's in your genes. You act all tough and jolly with your fancy neckerchieves and amusing gor-blimey trahsers but the minute you hear a cut-glass voice giving an order you roll on your back like a dog. And now, like a dog, you're going to die! See you arind, baby!"
"No, your majesty! Forgive me!" whined the cockernee.
BLAM! BLAM! BLAM! shat the gat.
BUDDA! BUDDA! BUDDA! BUDDA! BUDDA! BUDDA! barked the Uzi.
"AAAAAAAARGH!" screamed the spasming aquatic costermonger as the hail of steel-jacketed 9mm rounds thudded into his writhing body, tearing huge exit wounds in his back from which erupted violent geysers of jellied eel'n'lager-top polluted cockernee blood.

The door burst open and the three princes rushed in.

"Huzzah!" laughed the youngest prince. "The wicked witch is....*dead*?"

"Oh dear!" mumbled the heir to the throne as his mother, with that all-too-familiar pursed-lip look, pointed the still smoking Uzi at his pin-striped crotch.

"You boys have got some explaining to do!" she snarled.

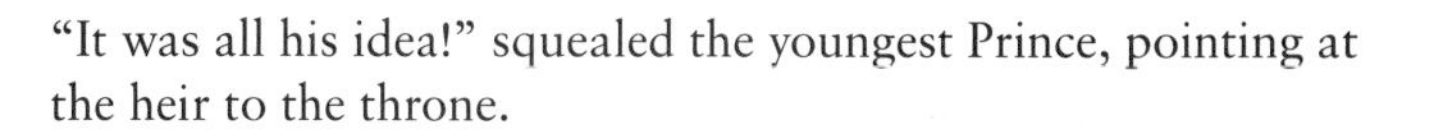

“It was all his idea!” squealed the youngest Prince, pointing at the heir to the throne.

Shut it, puff!” barked everyone else in unison.

“Faith is a living and unshakeable confidence, a belief in the grace of God so assured that a man would die a thousand deaths for its sake.”

Martin Luther, Preface to his translation of *St Paul’s Epistle to the Romans* .

CHAPTER 10

Billy Boyne and his chip-fed pig-featured Orangemen - so called because of their complexions - walked uncomfortably through the streets of Rome, BB himself looking at passing nuns with an I-smell-shite expression on his face while his cohorts studied at the examples of Papal idolatry that littered St Peter's Square.

"Holy relics!" shouted a vendor. "Get them here! Foreskin of Jesus! Fragments of the true cross! Threads from the Turin Shroud!"

"Haw!" grunted Billy. "Huv ye really goat Jesus's foreskin, pal?"

"Oh aye," said the vendor. "Loads o' them. Ye's want one?"

"Naw ya fuckin' Papish cunt!" spat Billy Boyne. He turned to his gang. "Ye's see? That's the Papes fur ye. Fuckin' Priest ridden superstitious cunts. That's why the reformation hud tae happen. We, as prodisents, don't believe any of that shite."

"Aye," said one of the gang members. "It's pish. God and Jesus and aw' that keech."

Billy Boyne slapped him hard.

"YA THICK CUNT!"

"Whit did ah say?" said the gang member, hurt and weeping.

"God isnae shite. It's aw the other stuff that's shite. Churches and the like," he barked.

The theological discussion drew to a close as father Ryan O'Brian left the office of the Holy Office, wiping blood off his hands with a rag.

"There's the cunt!" said Wee Fat Tam, ex Rangers Boys Club hooligan turned publican turned arch bigot.

"Jesus!" spat Billy Boyne. "That's that fuckin' IRA cunt we done a few years ago."

"Aye," said Billy Boyne. "The fuckin' same."

"So, haud oan Billy," said Big Fat Tam, brother of Wee Fat Tam. "How did the cunt manage tae get away that time?"

"Nae fuckin' time tae explain," said Billy producing his laser sighted Uzi 9mm from under his Kappa puffa jacket. "Intae him, ya bas!"

The crowds in St Peter's Square parted as the Prod Bigot Incompetents rushed the IRA Jesuit.
Father Ryan O'Brian was almost taken by surprise as the howling bluenoses came charging through the crowd, decked in Rangers strips and King Billy tattoos. Not a sight you saw every day in Vatican City.
"Aw, not youse lot again," he sighed, producing a heat-seeking surface to surface missile launcher and a Stanley knife from under his cassock.
BAM!
Six Prod-seeking Hereticbuster anti-bigot missiles took out six of the advancing bluenoses leaving only Billy Boyne and the surviving five Tam brother Wee Fat, Big Fat, Wee, Big and Fat.
"1690 YA BAS!" said Billy, machine gun blazing, Stanley knife flashing, cutting a bloody swathe through the nuns, priests and tourists.
Father Ryan O'Brian tossed the rocket launcher aside and taunted the Prods with a double alternating two-finger "fuck-you"waggle before running like fuck for the Vatican.
"Efter the cunt!" yelled Billy Boyne as they also charged into the Vatican.
The bloodiest battle that the Holy City had seen in many a year ensued as the bluenose terror squad fired and slashed at random, hacking off the privates of many a passing priest until a squad of crack Swiss Guard commandos arrived on the scene and began to shoot back. They were joined by squads of armed Poor Clares, a battalion of Neo Templars (the Vatican's zombie berserkers - lay priests brainwashed with mind control techniques learned over many centuries, reprogrammed as killers without conscience; as they had no souls left, they were not in any danger of going to Hell) and some crack-dealer Dominicans who kept Uzis under their cassocks to defend their turf against their hated rivals, the Jesuits. A well armed Jesuit unit also appeared; the Dominicans eyed them suspiciously. For a few moments it looked as though Billy's Boys were forgotten, that the war between the Dominicans and the Jesuits might

just hot up.
"Communist pig!" hissed Fr Manuel DeValera Pinochet Franco at the ascetic battle scarred Jesuit commander General Philip De Crevasse.
"Fascist filth!" retorted the Jesuit, looking with distaste at the epicene Dominican.
The stand off lasted a few seconds. Then General Phillipe De Cureversa SJ said: "For Christ?"
The Dominican nodded: "For Christ!"
They turned and unleashed a torrent of ecclesiastical hot lead. Billy Boyne and his incompetent Lodge Boys were soon holed up in one of the antechambers of the Vatican as the centuries old marble and plasterwork around them exploded with the rapid impact of white hot bullets; they were badly outnumbered and seriously outgunned.
General Phillipe De Cureversa SJ smiled sardonically as a sharpshooter from his Jesuit Commando unit took the head of one of the last surviving Glaswegian prods with a Desert Eagle. General Phillipe always smiled when he kicked the asses of would-be assassins who thought that the Vatican was a soft target. When Stalin quipped: How many tank divisions does the Pope have? the Jesuit general would have been able to retort: "Around 300, actually."
And now - the bomb!

The Jesuit troops who had killed members of the Orange hit squad received absolution from priests huddled inside battlefield confessionals.
Swiss Guards in their Kevlar armour and gas masks entered the building. Their leader nodded to De Cureversa who put a bullhorn to his lips and said: "Surrender and your lives will be spared."
Billy Boyne, his left arm shot off and his right a useless stump, fumbled with the pin of a fragmentation grenade. This was supposed to be a soft job; get in and do some priest in and fuck off back home with some duty free bevvy. The English

cunt never said anything about 400 odd Papes with state-of-the-art weaponry and bad attitudes.
He threw the grenade.
KAR-FUCKING-BOOOM!!!!
There were screams as armed priests and Swiss Guards were blown to fuck by the blast.
"NOSURRRENDAHHHYABAAAAAS!!!!" screamed Billy Boyne at the top of his lungs, standing up and firing off his 600 rounds-per-minute Russian-made AK 47 (which he'd bought offa retired legless mercenary just back from Croatia for £200) with his least totally fucked hand as best he could. A hail of Holy Roman hot lead tore him to pulp in seconds. The two surviving Glasgow thugs emerged from the smoke with their hands on top of their heads.
"We're awful sorry mister," said one of them . "It wasnae us."
"It was some bad boys that made us," said the other, uncertainly.
No prisoners," hissed De Cureversa, shooting him neatly through the forehead with a single shot from his Mach-10.

"In 1613 a bill was introduced into the House of Commons to compel Catholics to wear a red hat (as the Jews in Rome did) or parti-coloured stockings (like the clowns did), not only so that they could be easily distinguished, but also that they could be 'hooted at' whenever they appeared."

The Gunpowder Plot **by Antonia Fraser**

CHAPTER 11

“Excuse me, ma’am, but what are we to do with the princes?” greased Grand Master Samuel Wilberforce Of The Ancient Order Of Master Masons.

“Yes” said the Queen, “they’ve been very naughty boys.”

She turned to the three shamefaced and naked bluebloods who were trussed up in gaffa tape and hanging upside down from poles suspended from the Buckingham Palace ballroom ceiling.

The Queen looked at the gagged face of her youngest son.

“I’m very disappointed in you” she said. “So as a punishment I’m going to kill Mr Mittens.”

“Mmmmmf! Mffffffff! Mfffffffff! MmmmmmmMFFFFF! *MmmmmmmMFFFFF!*” protested the Prince under his gaffa tape gag.

The queen gently lifted her youngest son’s pet kitten out its carrying case and deftly slashed its throat open with a Stanley knife, throwing the twitching carcass to the ravenous corgis which, smelling blood, had come a’yapping around her sensibly shoed heels. Swiftly they tore it to pieces, crunching the delicate bones in their steel-tipped fangs and leaving a hideous trail of feline gore on the expensive carpet.

“We’ve also arranged for you to be married to a blonde bovine Sloane with her own PR company,” continued the Queen, licking the blood off her fingers, “and if you haven’t produced an heir within three years we’re going to have your willy cut off so you can’t put it up any more men’s bottoms.”

The Prince shuddered.

"And as for you two..."

The 100 year old Queen Mother entered the ballroom leading the leather-masked Prime Minister on a lead attached to rings that pierced his withered scrotum.

"Mummy's feeling frisky again."

Behind the gaffa tape, the princes screamed...

"I think God is silly because he should have painted everybody the same colour and then they wouldn't fight."

Ricardo, aged 7, quoted in Nanette Newman's Lots of Love.

CHAPTER 12

The proprietor of Herods lugged the last of three thermo nuclear warheads into the basement of the store, puffing because he was out of condition and already suffering from the early stages of radiation poisoning.

The warheads - conical, covered in Cyrillic script that read HAVE THE NISE DAY, KAPITALIST FILTH-DOGZ - were rusting and leaking and frankly Hassan had his doubts that they would actually work. Still, he took extra special care.

The last one in place, he sat back and caught his breath. He took out the medal awarded to him by the Knights of Gibraltar - a vulgar monstrosity the size of a small dinner plate - and polished it with the sleeve of his £800 pinstriped Armani-style suit.

He had proudly hung the photo of him receiving it from the Pope, who placed a friendly arm around his shoulders and gave a thumbs up for the camera, over his ornate desk so that it was the first thing that his staff saw when they entered his office to be racially or sexually abused. He had also met with all the Catholic powers of Europe; the rightful Czar of Russia, Big Nicky Romanov, currently working in a Coffee Republic - ironically - in Moscow; Jason Von Hapsburg, heir to the Austro Hungarian throne, currently lead guitarist in up and coming Digital Hardcore act FUCKPHASE 666; Za Za Bourbon, rightful Queen of France...such wonderful young people. And not at all snooty like their English counterparts.

He thought of the snub delivered to him by the Queen's husband the first time that they met.
And growled.

It was at an S&M shindig in Mayfair, in Madame Psychotica's world renowned Whacks Works where members of the aristocracy, the legal profession, movers and shakers in the city and broadsheet journalists went to have acid dripped on their testicles, watch much loved pet puppies being butchered by Madame Psychotica's crop-wielding rubber clad dominatrixes and to suffer the indignities and humiliations that are an expensive and acquired taste for English public school boys.

He was over in London for the first time, fresh from his camel buggering youth in the fetid docks of Tripoli, where times were so hard that he was often forced to dress as a lady in the hope of attracting passing trade from sailors.

The Queen's husband - he was immediately recognisable, even in a studded leather hood (the studs being on the inside) - was led in by Madame Trixie, the 25 stone one legged she devil in stilettos (or stiletto, as it happened - her solid latex pink rubber leg was only worn on special occasions) hopping before him, her hand firmly grasping the leash around his neck.

"On your knees, dogs!" she barked.

The cowed barristers, public school headmasters and Harley Street doctors dropped onto their heavily varicose veined knees, averting their eyes.

Hassan, enjoying the ministrations of Madame Wormwood, scrubber to the stars, a nonagenarian toothless hag in all over rubber, needle marks on her nose, which was the only part of her arthritic blue flesh that you could see, who flogged him with a toilet brush.

"Take that you wog bastard!" she said. "Try and imagine that I'm your mummy
doing this."

"Yes madam," grunted Hassan.

"I'm going to stick this right up your dirty fat arse," she cackled. "And you're going to love it."

"Oh, please, madam, no!" he said. "I really really mean it. I don't want....urp!...."

The bristles of the toilet brush scoured the inside of his sphincter,bursting his ringpiece in a bloody flux on the way up into his bowels. It was more painful than the time that the Islamic Brotherhood Of Hashishim -the bloody and feared secret society of assassins - left him staked out in the desert to be gang raped by wild dogs as part of their initiation ceremony. At least, that's what they had told him...

The Queen's husband was chained up beside him and Madame Trixie began to verbally humiliate him.

"You stupid greasy Greek fuck," she swore in a cockernee accent. "You know what's going to happen when the workers see how fucking lame you toffs are? They'll tear your fucking head off and stick it up your arse!"

"Ooh, yes please madam," quivered the consort of HRH. "Please stick my head up my arse!"

"SILENCE WRETCH!" she raked his naked back with a wooden paddle studded with fishing hooks. "I'LL DO WHAT I FUCKING WANT WITH YOU!"

Then she smiled.

"And right now I'm off for a cuppa!" she said. "Tea break, girls!"

The dominatrixes gratefully put down their whips, coshes, severed limbs, knives, dentist drills, castrating scissors, big sticks, anal-intruders,vibrating dildos and screwdrivers and tottered off for a well earned break.

"NOOOOOOOOOOO!!!!!!!" screamed the Queen's husband. "Nooooooooooooooooooooooooooooooooooooooooooo o!!!!Beat me! Whip me! Cut my cock off! Nail my balls to the floor! Shit on my fucking tongue!"

"I don't think so," said Madame Trixie, hopping off sadistically.

After the session, during which time the Queen's husband screamed in an agony of indifference, Hassan approached him.

"Hello, Mr Majesty," he said in his broken, obsequious English. "It is a great pleasure to make your acquaintance."

"Who the fuck is this dirty little dung trader," the Duke sneered. "Dinsdale!"

"Sah!" said a broken nosed secret service thug with a handle bar moustache and a toadyish working class Tory attitude.

"Keep this wog away from me."

"Certainly, sah!" said Dinsdale, whose sphincter itself seemed to be held to attention. "Oi! You! Paki! I'm on to you, son! You didn't see nothing, right? 'Is 'ighness the duke 'ere? 'E wasn't 'ere, right? You get me, woggo?"

"Please, honourable sir, I only wish to make the acquaintance of the honourable gentleman..."

"You do not understand, you 'orrible little fuckah!" screamed the ex-Sergeant Major. "You is scum, boy, and 'is 'ighness 'ere 'as better things to do with 'is time than talk to the likes of you. Now just fack off back to your fackin' camel or you'll be found floating face down in the Thames with your knackers in your marf, hunderstand?!!!"

Hassan nodded sheepishly, humiliated more thoroughly than at any time in his life before or since. And this was real humiliation - not the sort that could be bought off a London whore for the price of a half decent meal and a bottle of respectable wine at a semi-fashionable London restaurant. .

That had been in 1962 and yet it still seemed as fresh in his mind, as though it had been yesterday.

"Well, payback time for you now, Mr Queen," he laughed to himself. "Then we'll see whose knackers are in whose mouth."

"Hitler, Goebells, Himmler and most members of the party's 'old guard' were Catholics...It was not by accident that, because of its chiefs' religion, the National-socialist government was the most Catholic (that) Germany ever had...This kinship between National-socialism and Catholicism is most striking if we study closely the propaganda methods and the interior organisation of the party. On that subject, nothing is more instructive than Joseph Geobel's works. He had been brought up in a Jesuit college and was a seminarist before devoting himself to literature and politics...Every page, every line of his writings recall the teachings of his masters;

so he stresses obedience...the contempt for truth...'Some lies are useful as bread!' he proclaimed by virtue of a moral relativism extracted from Ignatius of Loyola's writings..."

L'Imperialisme Protestant **by Frederic Hoffet.**

CHAPTER 13

Disturbance over, the Pope emerged from his oxygen tent after receiving a complete blood change courtesy of the many orphans who visited him in VC. He felt invigorated and had the faint stirrings of a hard-on. It wasn't seemly for the Pontiff to go poking his pronger where it wasn't wanted, such as the anuses of young choirboys or the collapsing quims of octogenarian whores. Sometimes he envied the freedoms of the rest of the clergy. Still. Power was the ultimate thrill and as Pope - Christ's Vicar on Earth - he was still pretty fucking powerful, despite Vatican II, despite the best efforts of bloody John XXIII ("Idealists! Ugh!" he shuddered inwardly) and all notions of the Pope as being the servant of the church and not its master.

As a young priest in his native Lithuania, he had been intoxicated by the power that the Church wielded. He realised that.

He heard a noise behind him and started to turn...

Father Ryan O'Brian was being bandaged by a Swiss Guard field medic in the blasted corridor of the Papal ante chamber when the Pope walked in.

"Ah, O'Brian isn't it? Tell me, do you think it was me they were trying to kill ?"
"No, Holy Father" replied O'Brian, gesturing the medic away and shaking his bandaged head. "These comedians were a message. A sort of gentle smack on the wrists from them over in England. They know that we've got the bomb."
"And they'll know that we're prepared to use it to level London, yes?" said the Pope triumphantly. "Payback for Henry VIII and all that!"
"That's in place, your Holiness," said Ryan O'Brian. "But...."
"But nothing!" said the Pope, airily waving his hand in a gesture of dismissal. "Please don't bore me with the details."
"As you wish, Holy Father," genuflected the Irishman.
"And now, Father O'Brian. I'm afraid I must ask you to leave" said the Pope, tossing up his cassock and baring his hideously saggy arse to the still bowing IRA commander. "I have to attend a rather important meeting."
O'Brian obediently kissed the Pope's ring, inserting a tiny suppository made of super-concentrated Semtex and a microscopically small detonator and timing device as he did so. You can say want you want about the Swiss, thought Ryan, spraying his mouth as he left the devastated ante chamber, but they sure knew how to make a feckin bomb!

"When Kennedy read the Dallas Morning News on Friday morning, November 22nd, he was greeted by a full-page ad in bold, black type, suggesting he was a communist and a traitor. A few hours later, as he rode through downtown Dallas...the motorcade route was lined with posters picturing Kennedy with the words 'Wanted for Treason'. The stage was set for assassination."

Coup D'etat Trading Cards **by Paul Brancato**

CHAPTER 14

FBI Headquarters. Washington DC

"So you're thinking - who the fuck is this fat ugly old fuck in a

fucken frock? Am I right?" laughed FBI head honcho Edgar L. Ron Dyson. He was fat, ugly and wearing a frock.
"Um, yes sir, it had, er, crossed my mind..." mumbled recent FBI academy graduate Clarence T. Blackbird. He was thin, pretty and wearing a $1,749.99 Brooks Brother's suit, a crisply ironed Oxford button-down shirt and exquisitely hand tooled Patrick Cox calf-skin Chelsea boots.
"No fucken pun intended! Right?" barked Dyson. "See, the reason I'm wearing this here godamn fucken dress is because I'm a godamn fucken cocksucking, shit stabbing, jism-gobbling hard-core homofuckensexual transvestite fucken sexual fucken pre-vert. You got a fucken problem with that, boy?"
"Er, no..." mumbled Blackbird, his thin upper lip trembling, his high forehead beaded with sweat.
"Damn fucken straight you don't, muthafucka!" roared the top Fed, leaning across a desk littered with Barbie dolls in various stages of undress amongst several score well thumbed back issues of Power Tool Apocalypse and Hard Core Anal Holocaust. "And the fucken reason you don't fucken object, Mr fucken lardy fucken da little Lord fucken Fauntleroy fucken college boy faggot, is cos of THIS!"
Clarence Blackbird flinched as the thick manila file thudded into his lap. Then he gasped as he pulled out the top sheet - a top quality photocopy of a photograph of the aforementioned Clarence T. Blackbird dressed as Cabaret-era Lisa Minneli eagerly sucking on a sailor's brutally engorged love hammer whilst being simultaneously savagely stabbed up the shitter by a humungously over-muscled Mexican construction worker wearing nothing but a bright yellow hard hat and a pair of plastic tits .
"J-j-esus!" stammered the nervous neophyte.
"Shut your godamn blaspheming faggot mouth, boy!" snarled Dyson.
"D-d-d-oes this m-m-m-mean I'm f-f-f-f-f-f-f-f-f-f-f-f-fired?"
"Fuck no!" laughed Dyson, leaning back and scratching his Janet Reger clad crotch. "It means you're one of us, boy!" he

smiled, sniffing his incredibly pungent fingers. "Y'see every fucken schoolkid in the entire fucken US of fucken A knows that my esteemed fucken predecessor, Edgar J fucken Hoover, was a godamn muthafucken crossdressing player of the muthafucken purple-topped pink fucken oboe, right?"
Blackbird, his face pale with shock, nodded dumbly.
"But what folks *don't* know is that *ALL* FBI agents, right from the fucken beginning, have *ALL* been fucken beef-bayonet swallowing fucken fairies in fucken frocks! Fuck yes! We got the fucken idea from the Ancient fucken Greeks by fucken way of the godamn fucken Brits who, as you fucken know, only fucken recruit homosexual fucken communists into MIfucken5."
Blackbird gaped.
"Jesus muthafucken Christ on a fucken pogo stick, boy! Why'd'ya fucken think we fucken recruited your fucken sorry fucken ass in the first fucken place? Cos of fucken your godamn muthafucken good fucken looks? Ha! OK, here's the fucken deal. Matta fucken Hari? Real name Hershey P. Highway, a fucken FBI agent executed by the fucken French whilst on fucken secondment to the fucken Brits. Eleanor fucken Roosevelt? Real name Gerald O. Fitzpatrick, fucken FBI agent. Amelia Earhart? AKA fucken FBI agent Harvey F fucken Wooffenberger, shot the fuck down while filming Japa-fucken-nese fucken defence installations. Fuck, boy, the fucken look fucken on your fucken face! I fucken love this fucken bit! You fucken ain't fucken heard fucken nothing yet! George fucken Washington? Faggot! Samuel fucken Adams? Cockfuckensucker! Benjamin fucken Franklin? Fucken jism-guzzling sword fucken swallowing fucken cross-fucken-dressing fucken ass-fucken-biter! Fucken damn fucken straight! Fuck it!"
Dyson leant back in his chair, lit up a $900 Havana and studied the ashen features of his latest recruit.
"And now for the fucken big stuff. Fucken strap yourself the fuck in, boy, cos I'm fucken about to fucken blow your fucken mind!"

Dyson sucked in two massive lungfulls of pungent commie cigar smoke and blew out two perfect dollar signs, a trick he'd learnt off Fidel Castro (in reality FBI agent Cecilia B Oppenhiemer) herself.
"Fact fucken one. The fucken War Of fucken Inde-fucken-pendence? Fucken for-fucken-get about it! It fucken never fucken happened! The fucken whole fucken shooting fucken match was a fucken phoney fucken put-up job, fucken de-fucken-signed to fucken fool the fuck the fuck out of the real fucken enemy. Fuck! And you fucken know who the fuck that is, right?"
"Er, the masons?" offered Blackbird, timorously.
"Fuck no! Those fucken motherfucken cocksuckers!? Fuck! We fucken own their godamn fucken muthafucken fucken asses! For fuck's sake! Fuck no, boy, the fucken enemy! The *real* fucken enemy!"
"Um the Communists? Organised labour? The Illuminati? The Shriners? Er, Aliens? The Jews? The Irish? The Native Americans? The Democrats? The Australians? The Knights Templar? Vampires? "guessed Blackbird in increasing desperation. Dyson was right, his revelations had blown the poor bastard's expensively educated mind completely.
"No, no, no, no, no and fucken no!' laughed Dyson. "The fucken enemy, boy, is the godamn muthafucken anti-fucken-Christ! The fucken Whore of fucken Babylon!"
Ah, you mean, you mean...Madonna!" gasped Blackbird, his jaw almost hitting the tastefully carpeted floor.
"Holy fucken shit, boy! You fucken been fucken smoking that godamn fucken loco fucken weed! I fucken trained *that* fucken bitch myself. Her real fucken name's Chester D. fucken Patterson, ex fucken Navy fucken Seal, Medal Of fucken Honor winner and fucken damn fine fucken quarter fucken back to fucken boot! Fuck no, boy, I'm fucken talking about the fucken one and fucken only fucken godamn muthafucken fucken Catholic fucken church, boy! Fuck! You fucken wanna fucken know who fucken really fucken shot fucken Kennedy?

Huh? I fucken did! With a little fucken help from fucken Jackie, of course. Fuck yes!"
"Y-Y-You mean Jackie Kennedy was..."
"Real name FBI agent Basil H. Saunders, fucken popped the fucken asshole fucken twice with a fucken gun fucken hidden the fuck in his fucken hand-fucken-bag!" reminisced Dyson gleefully.
"Fuck! The magic bullet!" gasped Blackbird, otherwise utterly lost for words.
"You fucken wanna fucken know fucken why I'm fucken telling you this, boy?"
Blackbird gulped and nodded.
"You're fucken on the fucken A-Team, boy. From fucken now on fucken in you're a fucken 100 fucken per fucken cent fucken team fucken player on the fucken meanest, fucken scariest, fucken godamn fucken hardest fucken buncha fucken ruthless fucken muthafuckers, fucken mad-fucking-men and fucken stone fucken cold fucken assassins fucken ever fucken put to-fucken-gether in the fucken entire fucken glorious fucken godamn fucken history of the fucken godamn fuck fucken British fucken Emp-fucken-ire! Fuck! Shit! Asshole!"
"The *British* Empire?" gasped Blackbird, his tenuous grasp on reality slipping still further.
"Fucken fuck yes! The fuck! Fucken godamn fucken right, the fucken British fucken Empire!" roared Dyson angrily. "Fuck! Haven't you fucken been fucken listening to a fucken godamn fucken mutha-fucken-fucken fucken word I've fucken fucken fucken fuck fucken been fucken fuck god-fucken-damn fuck-saying!? Fuck it!?"

*

"Fuck! Haven't you fucken been fucken listening to a fucken godamn fucken mutha-fucken-fucken fucken word I've fucken fucken fucken fuck fucken been fucken fuck god-fucken-damn fuck-saying!? Fuck it!?"

The Pope nodded thoughtfully and steepled his delicately veined hands.
"So, this Blackbird, he is one of us, yes?"
"In a way, Holy Father" said Bishop Usher, head of the Vatican's feared Black Ops department. "Agent Blackbird has had several medical operations in the past few years, the result, I am afraid, of a rather severe car accident, enabling us to insert several pieces of extremely useful machinery into his various body cavities. Like the voice activated broadcast microphone we are listening to now, for instance."
"Well I never!" smiled the Pope. "Amazing!"
"More to the point, Holy Father," hissed Friar Sergei Flintov, one-armed and black eyepatch sporting supremo of the Latinate Internal Security Police, "I demand to know why *my* department wasn't informed of this operation!"
The Pope sighed. He knew that the Vatican's divide-and-rule policy of separating the Church's security arm into several score viciously competitive agencies was a tried and trusted success but still, he wished they wouldn't *bicker* so!
"Boys! Boys!" he cooed, as the Bishop and the Friar both instinctively and simultaneously whipped massive semi-automatic firearms out of their cassocks and levelled them at each others heads, causing a chain reaction of whipping out, aiming and cocking to ripple around the table which inevitably resulted in yet another dangerous and extremely tedious John Woo style mass Mexican Stand-off situation.
"Can I point out" purred the Pope, "that if you all start shooting we might miss something interesting?"
He gestured at the centre of the table where there sat a large purple speaker. From which emerged the unmistakable sounds of joyful man-on-man copulation.

*

"Mr Director, Sir!" yelled frizzy ginger-haired milk-bottle-

bottom-specced nerdy supergeek FBI Agent Wolf F. Molder as he burst into Dyson's office.
"Godamn it, Molder! Don't you ever fucken knock!" barked Edgar L. Ron Dyson as he lay naked and glistening with the gym-honed and still trembling body of the young Clarence T. Blackbird clasped tenderly in his incredibly hairy arms.
"We're sorry to bother you, sir!" purred svelte and sexy Special Agent Kenneth N Scally, pushing his geeky colleague out or the way and stepping into the room with all the cat-like grace of a major-league lead chorus girl stepping into the spotlight at Ceasers Palace.
"Blackbird! I wan'ya to meet Agents Molder and Scally!" snapped Dyson, (the first cuss-word free sentence he'd spoken in 3 months) leaping to his feet and wiping his still dripping cock on an American flag.
"M-Molder and Scally?" stammered Blackbird, hastily pulling on his now spunk stiffened Verscase boxers. "L-L-like in The X Files!"
"AH HA HA HA HA HA HA HA HA HA HA HA HA HA AH HA HA HA!" laughed Molder, Scally and Dyson conspiratorially. Like mad pirates.
"W-w-what's the joke?" mumbled Blackbird indignantly.
"Oh forgive us!" murmured Scally, sashaying up to Blackbird and gently cupping his youthful chin. "You see, Clarence , may I call you Clarence? Well, you see, Clarence, say, has anybody ever told you you've got beautiful eyes?"
"Fucken leave him the fucken fuck alone, you fucken bitch! He's fucken mine!" snarled Dyson, slapping Scally's hand away.
"Sorry sir, I didn't realise..."
"Yes, it's true. I fucken love the fucken sonovabitch!" snarled Dyson, turning to face his latest recruit with tears in his eyes.
Clarence Blackbird's superbly sculpted jaw dropped so hard it creaked.
"Yes, Clarence, it's true. I fucken love you. I've fucken loved you from the very first fucken minute I fucken clapped fucken eyes on that fucken photo of you choking on a swabby's fucken

pink torpedo whilst being simultaneously shafted fucken senseless by a fucken beaner in a fucken bright yellow fucken hard hat, you bastard!"

*

"I fucken love you. I've fucken loved you from the very first fucken minute I fucken clapped fucken eyes on that fucken photo of you choking on a swabby's fucken pink torpedo whilst being simultaneously shafted fucken senseless by a fucken beaner in a fucken bright yellow fucken hard hat, you bastard!"

"Do we know why the infidel swears so much?" asked Mother Clarissa of The Sisters Of Perpetual Vigilance, her chair placed on lots of newspaper to soak up the gunk that constantly streamed for the numerous leprosy sores that the top ninja-nun had contracted whilst working undercover in Calcutta as part of the Vatican's secret plan to brainwash as many Hindus as possibly away from the evils of pagan idolatry and into the arms of the Only True Mother Church.
"Well *we* do!" smugged Cardinal Ernst Dolfus of the Holy Ghostapo, primly. "We carried out DNA tests on a sample of the heretic Dyson's sperm which was discovered by one of my surgeon-agents operating on the ruptured stomach of a tortured and murdered young socialist boy during the unfortunate incident in Chile in 1972. The tests revealed, with a certainty factor of precisely 99.99999768% that FBI Director Edgar L. Ron Dyson is the one and only son of....."
The knife thin and ultra-blonde super-cop paused theatrically to dust a few non existent lumps of fluff off the silver death's head rune on the sleeve of his jet-black cassock.
"Her Majesty The Queen of England and her husband, The Duke!" yelled Dolfus excitedly, thumping the table with both of his heavily skull-ringed fists.
"And that explains the swearing!" gasped Brother Barrington Rapeman, head of the feared Papal Counter Intelligence Police.

"He's got Tourettes syndrome!" exclaimed Sister Veronica D'lisle, chief of the notorious Sisters Of Righteous But Inevitably Gratuitous Premature Retaliation.
"Just like his dear old dad!" laughed the Pope. "Amazing! Truly amazing! What a deliciously wicked world we fucking live in!"
"But, hang on," interjected Archbishop Raphael Maradonna, boss of the infamous Holy See Intelligence Agency (Domestic). "If this Dyson hombre is the only son of that pagan bitch and her fuckaddled bastard of a heretic husband, who are all the other sons and daughters that you see in the pictures in Hello magazine, eh?"
"Simple!" sneered the cold and calculating Dolfus, straightening a jet-black cuff and obviously revelling in the shock his bombshell had caused his rivals. "They are, in effect, not only not the children of the British monarch and her consort, they are not even, strictly speaking, *even human*!"
"What? They're fucking aliens?" gasped The Pope.
"No, Holy Father. Not quite. My spies in Buckingham Palace inform me that they are in fact organic constructs, Frankenstein's monsters if you will, put together at a secret British research laboratory in the 1940's using technology captured from the Nazis when British troops overran a certain concentration camp and stumbled across the horrific evidence of Himmler's deranged plan to replace the ever increasing German casualties on the Eastern Front with golems sewn together from the dead! Meanwhile, of course, the real prince was spirited away to America where it was thought that he would be forever safe from *our* tender mercies!"
"Yeah, dat kinda makes some kinda screwy sorta fucken sense!" drawled Monsignor Mikey 'No Nose' Mallone. Sicilian/American liaison officer for the Mid-West Costra Nostra. "Yous look at dat prince mudderfucka, da one dat talks to the fucken trees and fucks dat bitch with da face like da fucken horse and shit, yeah? Seems kinda fucken obvious dat dey stuck the fucken ears offa one stiff onta anudder fucken stiff's fucken head, yeah? Now you fucken think about

it!?"
"Exactly!" smugged Dolfus, glowing with pride.
"What? Get tae fuck! What a load of bollocks! He's just making this up!" jeered Padre Tam McKuckoldie, Grand Zulu Warrior Of The Ancient Papal Order Of Hardy Hibernian Zealots - a venerable Scottish Catholic institution which, ironically enough, had later mutated in America into the fiercely anti-Catholic Ku Klux Klan.
"I am NOT making it up!" roared the red faced Dolfus, pounding the table, stamping his jackboots and thus suddenly losing his carefully conceived air of icy blonde Aryan cool.
"Oh for God's sake!" groaned the Pope as another round of gun-brandishing clicked and clacked its way around the table. "Look, the rule is that we all do what Daddy says, right? Because I'm the Pope, OK? Yeah? Because I'm fucking in-fucking-fallible, remember? So Daddy says put the fucking guns away and sit the fuck down and let's all listen to this very interesting broadcast or I'll personally execute every holymotherfucking single one of ya! For fuck's sake!"

*

"Look, the rule is that we all do what Daddy says, right? Because I'm the Pope, OK? Yeah? Because I'm fucking in-fucking-fallible, remember? So Daddy says put the fucking guns away and sit the fuck down and let's all listen to this very interesting broadcast or I'll personally execute every holymotherfucking single one of ya! For fuck's sake!"

"So we're actually listening to a broadcast direct from the Vatican war room, are we, Colonel?"
"That's correct, madam!" slimed MI7 supremo Colonel Dalrymple Death-Saunders (pronounced Dee-arth Soon-duh-ears-ah) (retd.).
"How fascinating!" said the Queen, politely. "So, tell me, Mr Saunders, how long have you been head of my top secret

counter-counter-counter espionage organisation?"
"All of fifty years, madam!" said the spook, proudly.
"And do you enjoy it?" asked the Queen, sincerely.
She'd always had the most marvellous ability to make people feel at ease in her company. God bless her.

*

"B-b-but you *can't* love him!" gasped Wolf Molder.
"Why the fuck not?" snarled the still manfully sobbing Dyson, grabbing a whisky bottle, smashing it on the edge of his desk and waving it threateningly in the face of the cowering Wolf. "Because *you* fucken love him? Is that it? You sneaky fucken ginger bastard! I'll fucken kill ya! *Fucken kill ya*!"
"No, sir, please, it's not that, it's just that...that...."
"That fucken *WHAT*!?" screamed Dyson, the huge purple veins in his neck bulging like elephant cocks in a pachydermal porn flick.
"Because Agent Clarence Blackbird is in fact......"
"*FUCKEN WHAAAAAAAAAAAAAAAAAAAAAAAT!?!?*" screeched the puce faced Dyson, grabbing Molder by the throat and mere second's away from slicing and dicing the ginger agent's face into bloody dog food.
"*HE'S YOUR SON!*" screamed Molder in pant-shitting mortal terror.
"Wha....?" mumbled the suddenly limp and slackjawed Dyson. "H...he's my...son? My long lost son...?"
"Yes sir!" squeaked the hyperventilating Molder. "The child that was allegedly kidnapped by Palestinian terrorists when you were on Embassy duty in 1974 was in fact stolen from your tent by a pack of desert wolves who raised the child as their own until he was rescued by a passing caravan of Bedouin tribesman who later sold him to a couple of incredibly rich but tragically childless American tourists in Jerusalem, names of Mr Terrence V. Blackbird and Zena Y. Blackbird, who smuggled the kid home and raised him as their own! That's

what we were coming to tell you when we burst in here and discovered you, er, on the floor, um fucking your own son, ah, up the arse. Sir!"
"Are you fucken trying to fucken tell me that I've just fucken gone and fucken fucked my own fucken son up the fucking shitter?" said Dyson slowly.
"Sir, yes sir, Mr Director, sir!" woofed Molder.
"Fucken fuck!" murmured Dyson. And then he collapsed dead as his heart exploded with the shock.

*

"Shit, is he dead?"
"What the fuck just happened? Which one's dead? Is it Dyson or our man Blackbird?"
"Quick, call for an ambulance!"
"If you'd just shut up, maybe we'd be able to hear...."
"Forget the ambulance. He's gone."
"Don't you tell me to shut up, you bastard!"
"My father! Are you telling me that man was my father!?"
"Will you please all just shut the fuck up so we can hear what's going on!"
"'Fraid so, Agent Blackbird, it's all here in the file..."
"With the utmost respect, Holy Father, it's not me you need to tell to shut up. It's that cunt!"
"...and now he's dea.."
"ALL OF YOU FUCKING WELL SHUT THE FUCKING FUCK THE FUCK UP OR I'LL FUCKING EXCOMMUNI-FUCKING-CATE EVERY SINGLE FUCKING ONE OF YOUR FUCKING SORRY HOLYMOTHERFUCKING ASSES RIGHT FUCKING NOW! YOU CUNTS! YES, YOU TOO, YOU KRAUT COCKSUCKER! AND YOU, YOU WOG BITCH! I'M NOT FUCKING KIDDING! I'LL FUCKING DO IT! SO WHO FUCKING WANTS SOME, EH! WHO WANTS TO SPEND ALL ETERNITY IN HELL WITH THE PRODS, KIKES AND MUZZIES, EH? FUCKING EH? YOU FUCKING COCKSUCKING FUCKING WANKERS!!!!!"

"Deary me, what *is* going on?" asked the Queen, wrinkling her nose in confusion.
"Does this mean that this Blackbird chap is actually my only begotten grandson, Saunders? I must confess that I'm finding it all just a tad confusing."
"I think, your majesty," arselicked Colonel Saunders, greasily, "that the, ah - to use the, ah, North American vernacular - the ah, pooh is about to hit the old pukka wallah, so to speak.."

*

"OK! Let me try and get this straight" said Clarence Blackbird as he hastily pulled on his clothes.
"OK, so you're the real Molder and Scally and you work in a secret FBI department dedicated to subverting the Catholic church, your department being known as The Hex Files?"
"That's right!" purred Agent Scally.
"And the TV programme The X Files is just an incredibly clever piece of FBI planted disinformation designed to throw Joe Q. Public off the scent?"
"Correcto!" smiled Molder.
"And - let me see whether I understand all of this - the USA is merely the catspaw of the secret British Empire which, despite all evidence to the contrary, is still intact and, let's see, all human history since the 1500s has really been a result of the titanic death struggle between this British Empire and The Vatican for world domination, primarily in the form of a savage cold war over the world's drug and slave trades?"
"Right again!" slinked Scally.
"A bit player in this war being the FBI which, if I've got this right, is entirely staffed by insanely promiscuous homosexual transvestites of whom this man lying dead here was the leader as well, of course, as being my real biological father?"
"Got it one!" laughed Wolf Molder.
"And I've just fucked him? Fuck!" exclaimed Blackbird. "Fuck,

fuck fuck fuck fuck. This has fucking got to be the weirdest fucking day in my entire life!"
"This?" smirked Scally, kittenishly. "This is nothing! Welcome to the weird and wonderful world of the Hex Files, Agent Blackbird!

*

"Welcome to the weird and wonderful world of the Hex Files, Agent Blackbird!"

"And now, brethren" said Bishop Usher, "the moment you've all been waiting for!". And with that he pulled a small radio transmitter from his pocket, blew some fluff off it and pressed its tiny red button.
A loud **"KA-FUCKING-BOOM"** erupted from the speaker.
Fifteen seconds of total silence ensued.
"What" said Sister Ursula M'dingo, Mother Superior of the Sacred Sisters Of The Kung Fu Death Fist Made Sanctified Flesh, "was that?"
"That, dear sister," smirked the Bishop, "was the sound of the super-concentrated Semtex bomb my surgeons secretly implanted in Agent Blackbird's chest cavity exploding with extreme prejudice and killing everybody in the room thus ripping the very heart out of the FBI Hex files programme at a single stroke!"
"Oh well done!" drawled Father Charles Ripley-Worthington, Dojo Master of The British Catholic Warriors Of The Sacred Heart, laconically. "Well bloody done!"
"Thank you, Charles!" smugged the Bish.
"Although you might be ever so slightly interested to learn," continued the Brit, sardonically, "that Agents Molder and Scally, the very same people whom you have just so casually murdered, were in fact Catholic agents placed at the very heart of the FBI by *my* organisation, you bloody fool!"
"What?" gasped the Bishop. "Well how the hell was I supposed to know that? Why the fuck didn't you share that information,

you stuck-up, in-bred, pseudo-Catholic limey bastard!?"
Within seconds the Vatican war room was once again filled with deranged sectarian bickering which ended, of course, with yet another potentially lethal mass Vatican Stand-off.
"Ladies and Gentlemen!" cooed the Pope. "Brothers and Sisters!" he continued. "Ask yourself - what would the Baby Jesus be thinking if he could see us now, hmm? Which he can of course, being omnipotent and that, right? And his dear ole mum, Mary - what would she think, hmm?"
The gun-wielding clerics all looked at their feet, mumbled and turned red.. Slowly they stashed their gats back in their cassocks and sat down, thoroughly fucking ashamed of themselves.
"Now then," smiled the Pope, "let's put all this nonsense behind us. As our Good Lord said, no point crying over spilt milk, right?"
The assorted top Papal pigs all mumbled in shamefaced holy assent.
"Anyway, I have something much more important for you to see. Look at this!"
And with that The Pope pulled off the top of his left index finger to reveal a shiny red button. Which he started to press...
"No you don't, you feckin' arse!" yelled Father Ryan O'Brian, kicking the war room's ancient oak doors off their hinges, storming in and pressing s shiny red button all of his own.
KA-FUCKING-BOOM!
The Pope's arse blew clean off, killing him instantly.
"Fucking hell, O'Brian! You've just blown the Pope's arse off!"
"No I haven't!" laughed O'Brian.
"Yes you fucking well have!" chorused the rest of the room.
"No he hasn't!" said a figure suddenly appearing from the shadows behind O'Brian.
"Fuck me!" gasped Bishop Usher.
"It's the Pope!" gasped Father Charles Ripley-Worthington.
"Naked!" drooled Mother Clarissa of The Sisters Of Perpetual Vigilance.

"That's right!" exclaimed the real Pope, strutting into the middle of the room with his hands on his fat plastered hips. "The man that whose arse Father O'Brian has just blown off was a Protestant impostor put in my place when I was kidnapped and temporarily stashed in a broom cupboard by an elite SAS hit squad operating under cover of the farcical attack on the Holy See carried out by a bunch of deranged Orange militants."

"The Holy Father's right!" smiled O'Brian. "I suspected that the impostor wasn't the real Pope when I observed a lack of heroin needle pock marks on his arse. So I slid a Semtex suppository up his anus, organised a search of the entire Vatican, discovered the SAS hiding in a kitchen, organised their destruction, tortured the location of the real Pope out of the one survivor and - bish bash bosh - made it up here in time to stop that cunt gassing you all to feckin death with the nerve gas bomb he's got sewn into his chest cavity..."

"Thank God you're safe, Holy Father!" brown-nosed Bishop Usher.

"So who was the impostor?" asked Father Charles Ripley-Worthington.

"Well," smiled O'Brian, laconically. "Why don't we rip the arseless bastard's incredibly life-like latex mask off and see?"

*

"Oh dear! It does all seem to have gone a little pear-shaped, doesn't it, Colonel?" sniffed the Queen. "So, tell me, who was the valiant soul one's secret service managed to place in the Vatican. Some brave soldier, no doubt? Do we have a name. I'd so like to give the chap a posthumous VC."

"I'm afraid, ma'am, that I don't have the chap's name" grunted the MI7 supremo. "The Duke took personal control of the operation and kept it all rather hush hush."

"Yes, the Duke," mused the Queen. "Where is the Duke? One hasn't seen him arind for simply ages."

*

O'Brian ripped off the corpse's latex mask and tossed it aside. The creme de la creme of Papal piggery crowded around the corpse to get a good look at the real face of their would-be assassin.
"It's....him!" gasped Padre Tam McKuckoldie.

*

"THE DUKE!" screamed the Queen, thrashing like a mosher on Nazi Crank, ripping down curtains, punching holes in the walls and kicking corgis across the room in grief and anger, "Oh my darling!" she wailed. "My darling little Stavros! What have they done to you?! What have they done to you!?"

*

"Fucking let me through for a looksie!" snarled the naked Pope, elbowing his way through the cassocked mob.
"Stick me inna fucking broom cupboard, willya, ya CUNT!" he snarled whilst viciously stamping the deceased Duke's face into pulp with his bare foot.
"RIGHT!" he roared, leaping up on to war table and dancing lie an E-overdosed teen in his rage and his fury. "Right! That's fucking IT! I've had it with that fucking BITCH! We've pussy footed with these bastards long ENUFF! Well that's fucking IT! She's just made it fucking PERSONAL! It's time for OPERATION NEW ARMADA! This time we go ALL THE WAY! This time we..."
And then he clenched his podgy fist, raised to the heavens and let out a inhuman scream that sent the millions of bats roosting in the Vatican belfry streaming out into the night in a frightened frenzy.
"This time we....*NUKE LONDON*!"

*

"Colonel Saunders," said the Queen, who had by now fully regained her well bred composure. "Would you be so kind as to ring for a servant and ask him to fetch one a pen and paper?"

"Dear Prime Minister" wrote the Queen in flawless copperplate.
"Here are your orders for today. They've killed my husband and only child.
So nuke Rome.
Yours sincerely,
HM The Queen

"The danger the world is exposed to because of this Company is far greater today than...when the two World Wars broke out. No one can nurse any illusions as to the deadly consequences another conflict would have."

The Secret History of The Jesuits
by Edmond Paris

CHAPTER 15

"No, ma'am, I'm not saying that we can't flatten the Vatican with every single nuclear missile in the entire NATO alliance" sighed the Prime Minister. "I'm merely suggesting that such action might be considered - how shall I put this - a tad rash?"

*

"Er, are you sure about this, Holy Father?" said Father Ryan O'Brian. "No that I'm doubting your total infallibility or anything but, y'know, nuking a city of 10 million souls into radioactive slag? Isn't that a bit, well, y'know, OTT?"

*

"Listen, you hair-lipped, cock-sucking, shit-gobbling, arse-fucking piece of greasy shit dago bastard! I am the Queen!" spat the Queen. "And as such I can do anything I fucking like, right?"
"Well, yes, in theory..." said the Prime Minister.
"No!" yelled the Queen angrily. "Not "in theory"! In. Fucking. *FACT!* Those papist bastards have butchered the only man I have ever loved and murdered the heir to the British throne! Do you understand? I want them dead! Every single fucking one of them! Dead! Dead! Dead! *FUCKING DEAD*!"

*

"O'Brian!" snarled the Pope. "Are you questioning the will of God? Because that's what you do when you challenge John fucking Pope, you know that don't you?"
"Of course, Holy Father!" yelled O'Brian, snapping to attention.
"Then what the fuck is your problem, Paddy?" spat the Pope, his huge dick swinging like a heavily veined mechanically-reclaimed meat pendulum as he strode back and forth across the Vatican war table like a man possessed.
"I was merely trying to point out, Holy Father, that the two Russian nukes we've smuggled into the top people's shop Herods are *tactical* weapons."
"Meaning what?"
"Meaning that they make a little bang, rather than a little bang, relatively speaking" explained the IRA man.
"So what are exactly are you saying?" asked the Pope, his huge, fat plastered body still trembling with murderous rage.
"Well, Holy Father, if we were to wait until after the Royal visit to top people's shop Herods, which is scheduled for

tomorrow afternoon..."
"I'm listening..." snarled the Pope.

*

"Oh, Stavros!" sobbed the Queen. "What have they done to you? What have they done to my beautiful Greek Adonis!"
"Love you too, darling! Anyone seen the bally fox? Tally ho! Pip pip! Wogs ahoy! Arooga arooga! Take two bottles into the shower? I should fucking co-co!" quipped the by now totally Tourettes-addled Duke, dressed as Mussolini in a pink ballet tutu and riding into the ornate throne room on a sturdy palomino polo pony.
"D-d-d-ukey!" stammered the Queen. "You're alive!"
"Last time I looked, sweetcheeks! Got any straight bananas? Is that a Paki in your pocket or are you just pleased to see me? Coons in the cupboard? Nice one, Cyril!"
"B-b-but I don't understand!" sobbed HRH, "Weren't you just offed by the Papists?"
"Oh that?" laughed the Duke, swatting imaginary flies with his riding crop. "That was just a lookee-likee, ploy to throw Johnny Wop off the scent, no offence intended, Prime Minister, you donkey-fucking dago bastard! This carpet looks like it's been shat on by a Hindoo with the arse of an elephant, no offence intended to our cat-eating wog cousins of course. Have you ever fucked a chink for a fiver, Prime Minister? I have. Cunts go sideways you know. *And* they *stink* of marmalade!"
"Now look here, Pater!" interrupted the heir to the throne angrily. "What's all this rot mummy's gotten into her silly head about us three being Frankenstein's monsters and some bally yank poofter being the real heir to the bally throne?"
"Is that a fly on your face, big ears?" asked the Duke, savagely slashing his eldest son across the left cheek with his crop. "No? Thought not. That's rot too. Total bollocks. All part of my cunning masterplan to feed Johnny Left-footer so much

bullshit he won't know whether he's coming or going. My dog's better than your dog! Is it real life or is it Maybeline? Yoiks! Bloody hell, wifey, you should know! You gave birth to the fuck-ugly little bastards! Must have been like shitting the fucking FA cup with this big eared cunt, what? Did you year the one about the wog, the chink, the wop, the dago, the spic, the spaz, the flid, the mong, the kraut, the frog, the lezzer, the paki and the nigger who go into a chemist and try and buy a packet of condoms so they can rape this beautiful blonde white woman? Anyway, the chemist's a yid, right, and..."

"Can I assume, ma'am, that you won't be needing those nukes after all?" asked the PM, discreetly.

"Well, I suppose not." said the Queen primly. "But keep them handy, Prime Minister. I have a feeling that we'll be using them sooner rather than later...."

"SHE KILLED MR MITTENS!" shrieked the youngest Prince, staggering into the throne room dressed in a tight little Victoria 'Posh Spice' Beckham style Versace black leather mini-dress and clutching a tiny teddy bear, tears causing his heavy mascara to run down his heavily rouged cheeks.

"Shut it, it you puff!" roared everybody else.

"You ruined my fucking punchline, you lisping little nancy boy!" roared The Duke, slashing his youngest son repeatedly about the head and chasing him squealing out of the room. Everybody else laughed uproariously.

What a family! thought the Prime Minister.

They made him proud to be *British!*

"The air is dusty with traffic haze. Most of the city's inhabitants are holidaying in the South. The sultry weather promises thunder, but not the kind that is to come later that night with the impacted force of a Mercedes 280-S limo crashing at high speed into the thirteenth pillar of a Paris underpass."

Diana - The Last 24 Hours by Allan Silverman

CHAPTER 16

ERUMPH!

The afterburner in The Duke's Rolls Royce 500,000 CC aircraft-engined Hawker-Siddley Blitzspear belched purple flame as it sped the totally bald super-xenophobe through the top secret 'Royals Only' super-motorway that ran under the Thames.

"Fucking spic chutney! Piccaninny killer comin' atcha, muthafucka! Look out woggy boy, it's death in a Flat fucking Eric mask! Who is the cunt eared jug-daddy? I am the jug-eared cunt-daddy! Oh yeah! Say it again! Ten tons of liquid steel and a righteous fucking need to kick towelhead arse in my achey-breaky heart and a mind to do malice to the enemies of the crown! Down boy! Wa's ma name? I said - WA'S MA NAME! The name's cunt! King Kunt! Oh yes! Fuck yes! Cunt yes! Death yes! Yes in-fucking-deedy-bastard-cunting-fucking doody-roody-diddly! BASTARD! Born to kill! Born to rule! Ace of spades! Ace of spades! Look out, a partridge! *BAM ! BAM! BAM!*" screamed the Duke, giving full vent to his ever worsening Tourettes as he flicked a toggle on the Blitzspear's endangered species skull encrusted dashboard that caused the fucking brilliant 'Extrmntr' album by the fucking awesome Prml Scrm to come blasting out of the Blitzspear's discreetly hidden speakers.

"*Swastika Eyes! Swastika Eyes!*" roared the Duke as he switched on the cruise control, whipped out a copy of *The Shooting Gazette* and started to wank. 'Swastika Eyes' spoke to the Duke on a deep spiritual level and that's why, when driving, he always wore a pair of aviator Ray Bans with crude white swastikas scrawled on the lenses in Tippex. Like he did now.

"Here he comes! Get ready!" spat self styled Sheikh Hassan I Sabbah Abdul Al Hazred, owner of the sprawling and ancient Herods department store, to his assembled minions as the Royal Blitzspear span to halt in the top secret underground car port which the Royals traditionally used when visiting Herods.
"Evenin' all!" roared the Duke, as he emerged from the cockpit with a fully cocked automatic pump action shotgun in each hand.
BAM! BAM! BAM! BAM! BAM! BAM! BAM! BAM! BAM! BAM! coughed the superbly balanced Browning shotguns, blasting Hassan's elite bodyguard into piles of twitching dog food.
SPLAT! PLAT! PLIP! and *PLOP!* went huge bloody chunks of the bodyguard's bodies as they splattered all around.
"Pull!" yelled the Duke out of sheer force of habit.
"Ah, good evening, your Royal Highness!" grovelled Hassan, bowing low.
"Wotcha, wog!" grinned the Duke, unsheathing a 6ft long claymore sword and advancing on the embarrassingly servile shopkeeper.
"Have you seen my new medal, sir?" inquired Hassan, pointing to the huge silver star set in a sea of diamonds and rubies that was suspended across his chest by a wide and incredibly vulgar puke-yellow silk ribbon.
The Duke looked. It was a mistake. Hassan whipped a massive gold handled scimitar out from behind his back and attacked.
SWIIIIIIIIIIIIIIIIIIIIIIIIIIIIIIIIIIIIIIIIIIIIIIIIIIIIIIIIIIIIIISH!
Only the demented spastic twitching that was a side-effect of his incurable Tourettes saved the Duke as he spasmed to one side suddenly and Hassan's scimitar sliced off his left ear.
"It's very nice!" said the Duke sarcastically as a geyser of bright blue blood erupted from the side of his shiny head.
Unsupported on one side, the swastika Ray Bans now

awkwardly hung across his dementedly grinning and gore spattered face, making him look even madder than he actually was.
"What did you get it for? Services to camel fucking? And one doesn't wish to be rude, Mr Hassan, but it really isn't the done thing to wear brown shoes with black trousers, YOU CUNT! *YEEEEEEAAAAAAARGH!"*
The Duke's claymore swung in a vicious arc vectored on Hassan's head.
"Aaaaaaaaargh!" screamed Hassan, incredibly embarrassed about the shoes, as he instinctively leapt backwards so that the brutal blade only succeeded in ripping out his madly staring right eye.
Hassan staggered, disorientated by the fact that the brutally removed eyeball was dangling down his corpulent cheek, still attached by the stringy bits. His pain maddened brain was thus confused by the contradictory visual signals it received.
"No, it's the Star of the Papal Order Of The Knights of Gibraltar, actually, sir" pointed out Hassan, slicing through the stringy bits with his scimitar, popping the now useless eyeball in his gob and chewing and swallowing it.
"*Traitor*!" screamed the Duke, leaping to the attack.
"*Snob*!" roared Hassan, rushing forward to avenge his social humiliation.
CLANG! CLANG! CLANG! CLANG!
Scimitar and claymore clanged, flashed, thrust and parried. Sparks flew. The combatants previously witty repartee ceased - to be replaced with a series of barely intelligible animalistic grunts.
CLANG! CLANG! CLANG! CLANG!
Finger tips, bits of cheek and nose and geysers of hot red and blue blood whizzed through the air as the two demonically energised warriors simultaneously sought lethal advantage. It was like the crusades all over again. On CRACK!
CLANG! CLANG! CLANG! CLANG! SHIIIIIIIIIIIIIK!
The Duke's superbly muscled left arm fell to the floor with a

sickening slap.

CLANG! CLANG! CLANG! CLANG! KLUNK!

Hassan's scimitar snapped clean in two as the claymore continued on its murderous course, hacking Hassan's lower jaw from his screaming face.

The storekeeper panicked, turned and ran. Straight into a wall.

THUD!

When Hassan came to the Duke was stood over him, the vicious claymore held over his head. He was dribbling, rolling his eyes and singing 'Onward Christian Soldiers'. With added swearing.

Hassan rolled on to his knees, clenched his bloody and increasingly fingerless hands together in front of him and proceeded to beg like a dog. A jawless dog.

"Ugkkk kkkukkaph uk uuk ak!" he spluttered, uselessly.

The Duke stopped singing. His mad staring eyes suddenly seem to focus and unglaze.

"Ah, Mr Hassan! There you are!" he said, as if suddenly noticing the cringing faith-traitor for the first time.

"Ikugh akugh okkle ak!" grovelled the doomed storekeeper pathetically.

"Yes, I see." said the Duke. "But I'm afraid that I'm here to see you today on an entirely unrelated matter."

"Afgahg ickle gurgle urhg ockkle grockle ik ak ok!" pleaded Hassan desperately.

"What? My sunglasses?" said the Duke. "Yes, they are rather good, aren't they? Made them myself you know, How nice of you to notice. But to the matter in hand. I'm afraid I'm here to day to ask that you remove my Royal Warrant from your store front. It's all those nasty lies you've been spreading about me, Mr Hassan. It really won't do, you know, going around telling people I'm some sort of swivel eyed racist monster. Terribly bad form!"

"Urk ik aggle orgah gibble gah!" screamed Hassan in one last desperate attempt to throw himself on the Duke's tender mercies.

"That's "urk ik aggle orgah gibble gah, *sir*!" to you, ya cunt!" snapped the Duke as he raised and lowered the claymore again and again and again, hacking the still desperately genuflecting Hassan into Mince Morsels (tm) sized cubes of still spasming rat food.

Trembling with blood lust and violently jerking in a demented spastic parody of an E-overdosed tekno-raver's last ever epileptic fit as his semi-reptilian mutant Royal DNA began the slow and incredibly painful re-growth of his missing, arm, nose, ear and finger tips, the Duke tossed back his gore-spattered head and let out the ancient victory cry of the British Royal Family.

"UUUUU

UUUUUU

UUUUUU

UUUUUU

UUUUUU

UUUHAAA

AAAAAAA

AAAAAAA

AAAAAAA

AAAAAAA

AAAAAAA

ARGH!

YOU

CUNTZ!"

Fifteen stories above this scene of sickening carnage, the crudely made, badly installed and amateurishly wired timer in one of the rusty and aged ex-Soviet tactical nukes malfunctioned.
Kensington High street was awash, as usual, with the designer clothes clad scum of the earth. Hideously ugly nouveau-riche matrons in hideously ugly Chanel outfits rubbed shoulders with the chinlessly honking offspring of Britain's genetically defective landed aristocracy. Alice-banded It Girls sipped £3.50 a pop cappuccinos with their extremely punchable floppy-fringed Old Etonian boyfriends (who all had girl's names like Hilary). Jeep driving and green Puffa jacketed repressed lesbian wives of repressed homosexual Tory MP's jostled for space with Aston Martin driving trustifarian half-wits and double decker buses chocka with gawping tourists.

The bomb detonated.

The Duke's Royal Warrant disappeared from the front of Herods.

The front of Herods disappeared from Herods.

Herods disappeared from Kensington High Street.

Knightsbridge disappeared from the map of London.

The carnage was terrible. The loss of life staggering. The resulting human suffering utterly incalculable.

Oh dear. What a pity. Never mind.

"War is stupid/and people are stupid..."

Boy George

CHAPTER 17

The missiles flew.

Rome died screaming.

Thousands of revenge-crazed prisoners emerged from the Inquisition's shattered cellars.

Thousands more from the ancient catacombs.

Like a black tide they spread across Rome, butchering nuns and priests and burning churches.

The 2000 year old Catholic Church collapsed under the

onslaught.

"Bigotry may be roughly defined as the anger of men who have no opinions."

Heretics **by G.K. Chesterton**

CHAPTER 18

ONE YEAR LATER. GLASGOW.

Easterhouse is one of Glasgow's less desirable housing schemes; originally designed after the war as a concentration camp for the city's soon to be redundant urban proletariat, Easterhouse had now become a sort of farm for the aristocracy.

As you know, the British aristocracy - like all the inbred aristo dynasties of Europe - are cannibals; it's the one thing that marks them off from the social climbing nouveau riche.
A beastly self-made little man who made a pile in bin liners or disposable tampons or telecommunications, say, could turn up to the hunt and stuff himself with rancid pheasant, but they all - no matter how badly they want to pass themselves off as one of the nobs - balk when the steaming corpse of a murdered

lumpen prole child with an apple stuffed in its mouth is set down before them. They may steel themselves to fuck and murder children, but few can really bring themselves to actually eat them. And that's why the Royals and their aristocrat lickspittles have always ruled over them with such unyielding and unquestionable authority.

Easterhouse is where the best human meat for the British blueblood tables comes from; like fois gras, they like them fed to bursting. They like the taste of flesh that has gone slightly necrotic and hence encourage the Glasgow diet of deep fried pizza, Mars Bars and chips washed down with Eldorado wine, Tennants Extra and high sugar Irn Bru. Connoisseurs of the long-pig will tell you that unless human flesh is diseased, it has little real flavour. Children are eaten as starters, but it's felt that they taste rather bland and need heavy sauces and spices to make the palatable. Adults - particularly the 60 fags a day adults who live on a diet of deep fried pizzas and salt, who never take any exercise and whose bodies are possibly riddled with tumours - are considered a real delicacy. As the arteries harden and the blood pressure drops, the pale, blubbery flesh of the unemployed Glaswegian begins to rot. And it's at this point that they are harvested.

But they also use them for sport...

Big Davey Murdoch hadn't been out of the house for nearly a week, not since he'd waddled down to the boarded up post office to cash his giro. The money was all gone now - spent on bevvy, fags and deep fried food from the last surviving Easterhouse chippy - and he was shitting it because he owed large to local moneylender Big Tam Wilson.

And today the money was due.

Big Davey had never worked and had soon grown as big as a

house, his greying blue flesh scored by festering indian ink tattoos that read KING BILLY and RANGERS FC YA BAS and 1609 FTP and GOD SAVE THE QUEEN. Big Davey was glad that the Pape and his whores had been obliterated in the recent war. He'd cheered when the police had arrived to cart his Catholic neighbours away to "re-education camps". He'd cried with pride the day the Queen had announced on telly that Britain was now a Fundamentalist Protestant state and that sexual deviance, socialism, liberalism and all belief in all other religions - but especially Catholicism - were now capital offenses punishable by being burnt alive at the stake. The good old days were back - with a vengeance!
Because Big Davey Murdoch loved his Queen! God Bless her! And now the world was perfect. Except that it wasn't, was it? Big Davey's life was still shit. Dimly, at the very back of Big Davey's bigotry deranged and patriotism deadened brain he harboured the faintest suspicion that maybe - just maybe - everything he'd ever believed in was total bollocks. That maybe his real enemies hadn't been the Catholics and the homosexuals, the pinkos and the reds. That his real enemy - the ones that had kept folk like him in the gutter for centuries - were the ruling class. A ruling class led by none other than his much beloved Queen herself.
But Big Davey's embryonic gropings towards a primitive class consciousness and thus towards a fully-fledged understanding of the essential truth of the Marxist dialectic were never to develop into anything more substantial.

He had mere minutes to live.

At eight am the door went. Literally. None of that knocking crap for Big Tam. He came in with a battering ram and his six rottweilers - Adolf, Heinreich, Joseph, Herman, Reynhard and Eva - came screaming into the bare council house barking and slobbering all over the denuded floorboards. Big Tam had had their teeth replaced by steel ones, razor sharp death-fangs that could chew through a screaming human face in less than a second. He injected them with crystal meth so that they were no longer merely dugs; they were quivering manifestations of raw hatred, barely controllable and ravenous for meat.

Big Davey, five foot five and weighing nearly 28 stone, dressed in a string vest and yellowing white Y-fronts, cowered in the far corner of thc living room. There was no furniture in the flat and the public utilities had been cut off months ago. The walls were papered with old copies of the Evening Times and because the bog was stopped up with concrete (he had stolen a load one night and tried to flush it away when the police came round) he had had to improvise a sort of litter tray for himself to shit and piss in. The house smelled vile.

Big Tam glowered. "The money?"

"Aye...er...ah'm...gist..." Big Davey quivered like an obscene lump of white jelly.

"Aye? Naw?"

"Er.....nnnnnnn.....naw," he said. "But I get mah giro next week."

"You owe me £100,000 ya cunt," said Big Tam. "Ah take it yer giro's no' gannae cover that?"

"Bit ah only borrowed twenty quid!" he whimpered.

"Interest, son," said Big Tam. "It a' mounts up."

"Aw, gies a brek, man!" said the fat man.

"Aye," said Big Tam. "Awright."

He looked at the fat cunt's GOD SAVE THE QUEEN tattoo and smiled broadly.

Then he knelt down and stared the quivering white trash in the blubbery face.

"Aw ye have tae dae is make it tae the road an' ah'll let ye aff."

"Whit, nae jokin'?" said the quivering mass of maggot white Glaswegian unemployable male.

"Aye, ah'll even gie ye a five minute head start," he said, looking at his watch. "Startin'...now!"

Big Davey didn't need to be told again. He climbed unsteadily onto his feet, bolted past the snapping dogs and squeezed out the door, past Big Tam's hard-faced henchmen armed with crowbars and clawhammers, down the glass strewn stairs in his bare feet and out, half naked, across the concourse where abandoned cars and rusting fridges lured local kids to their deaths. The thugs laughed their arses off as he went - the obese lumpen-prole bastard was puffing well before he'd gone ten feet from the smashed-in front door.

"Gawn! Run ya fat cunt!" they laughed.

The Hunt received their cue by mobile phone.

They waited in the shadows underneath the mouldering council block. Mounted on horseback. Twenty reptilian, thin lipped, jug eared, chinless. pigeon chested, transparent skinned, flush-cheeked, near-albino bluebloods - literally - all of whom could trace their family trees back hundreds of years before the Norman Conquest to the ancient cannibal dynasties of Gaul and Germania.

“Tally ho!” said the master of hounds, unleashing a pack of crack demented pit bulls, all raised on a strict diet of human flesh and starved for a week before the hunt. The gang of inbred aristocratic weirdos followed on horseback, dressed not in the red livery of the fox hunt, but the older black clothes of the Wild Hunt whose tradition went back to the pre-Roman rulers of ancient Europe.

The people of Easterhouse knew that it was best to stay indoors when the hunt was out. Unlike fox hunting, prole hunts never attracted protesters; who, after all, would feel any sentimental attachment to overweight unemployed Glaswegians?

Big Davey ran surprisingly fast for an extremely fat bloke, which delighted the braying mounted hunters who were used to catching their quarry in a few seconds. The dogs made no noise other than an eerie snuffling as they bolted in unerring straight lines, their bodies a solid contusion of muscle and stomach, driven insane by the thought of sinking their huge fangs into the succulent flesh of the fat man running away from them.

The riders steered the clumsy horse through the still dark winter morning, over broken bottles, needles and syringes and shattered TVs and the odd supermarket trolley that littered the ground around the estate.

All the riders wore leather hoods, though these weren’t any cheap junk that you bought from some Soho leather queen shop; these were hand-crafted from well-cured human skin.

Big Davey - exhausted after less than three minutes running - saw the road through the chain link fence and knew that if he made it that far, he was free.

Only a few more yards....

Even though he had no life, merely a pointless existence, Big Davey feared death by dog frenzy more than anything in the world. As a child he had watched in terror as a mad alsatian had run into the school playground, picked up his wee brother in its jaws and shook him to death. The dog was caught and was about to be put down when a local newspaper whipped up a campaign to have "Satan" reprieved. Pensioners and bourgeois do-gooders organised a hunger strike outside the local RSPCA and eventually the authorities relented. What, after all, was the life of one more sub-human snot-nosed chip-eating low IQ unemployable piece of human trash in Glasgow to the life of a dog that had probably been cruelly treated?

Big Davey ran. The dogs snapped at his heels. There was a tear in the fence that he used to take a short-cut to the bus stop.

Only a few more yards....

"Ah nae! *Ah fuck!*"

They'd boarded up the opening in the fence. In a deaf, dumb and blind panic, Davey looked around for another way out... He tried half heartedly to climb the fence. Too late. The first dog chomped his left leg right through to the bone. Davey screamed inhumanly until another dog fastened its jaws onto his face and ripped it off along with his tongue and voicebox. Then another at the throat and another and another...until all that remained was a huddle or writhing dog muscle, slavering and snarling as they tore the mercifully dead fat Glasgow prole apart, limb from limb - literally.

The hunt arrived in time to see the scene and cooed with delight. For some, including the young princes - the sons of the heir to the throne - it was the first kill that they had ever witnessed. But for the others - while the thrills of unnatural sex, unnecessary displays of power and exotic drugs quickly lost their allure - the thrill of watching the lower orders being savagely torn apart by vicious dogs was evergreen.

"Save some meat for us!" laughed the leader of the hunt to the master of hounds.

"Very good, b'wana," said the master, tugging at his forelock.

The dogs were tranquillised, pulled off and muzzled by the gang of hunt followers who had arrived in the wake of the horses. There was still lots good eating left on Big Davey.

The two Royal Princes were taken to the corpse and blooded; their photos were taken holding up the swollen, sclerotic, still warm heart, steam rising into the freezing cold air of a typically brutal winter's morning in the shit part of Glasgow. Servants brought up pints of porter for the overstimulated huntsmen - some of them openly masturbated over the corpse. Others were serviced by local children who were drugged and brought by their parents who were paid in Maundy money.

A marquee had been erected and the hunt dismounted for a fine breakfast. As well as the man they had hunted, other fat council tenants who had been butchered earlier by a local hospital were served up.

The Butcher Royal examined the marbled white flesh of Big Davey with a professional eye and began carving it into strips to be served rare and bloody on polished silver platters. The blue bloods - chinless, pale and with the small dead black eyes of chickens - held up the strips of flesh and allowed them to slither deliciously down their throats, slowly and exquisitely, tasting the metallic tang of blood mingling with the raw-pork flavour of the blubber. They began swapping stories of other hunts and remarking on the quality of Glaswegians as opposed to, say, Tynesiders or - worse - the Irish, who were generally considered too stringy and tough.

The two young princes gnawed contentedly on shin bones. It was, they agreed, the perfect start to any day.

"You there, oik! Fetch one some facking Sunny D!" honked the elder of the two young princes at a hovering equerry.

"Certainly, sir!" muttered the minion, stepping forward, head bowed and carrying a silver tray supporting two golden goblets full of the popular and delicious semi-fruit drink balanced elegantly on one gracefully poised white gloved palm.

The young princes quaffed the D with gusto.

And then choked, turned purple and started to die.

Panic rippled through the ranks of the hunters as a vile pink froth started spewing from the princes' spasming gobs. Screams rent the marquee as putrefying organs burst through the lads' rapidly blackening skins, whizzed through the air and then exploded, spraying the panicking mob of blue bloods with yet more of the Ebola 3000 super-bug with which the young prince's soft drink had been craftily contaminated.

Father Ryan O'Brian chuckled to himself as he stripped off the borrowed servant's uniform and kicked his chopped Harley superhog into screaming life.

So the Prods thought the war was over, did they? Ha! It had barely started!

"He discovereth deep things out of darkness, and bringeth out to light the shadow of death."

Job, 12:22
Quoted in *The Tower Of London Memorial of the Powder Treason.*

CHAPTER 19

November 5, three years later. A Royal Garden party.

"Hello. And what do you do? How interesting. How long have you been doing it? Really, how fascinating. Did you have far to come today?"
"Oh for heaven's sake! It's me, mummy! Your eldest son!"
"Are you enjoying the unseasonably mild weather? Have you tried the baked potatoes yet? One hears that they're terribly good!"
"It's no good, Jug Ears, the old bat's gone total remote control!" barked the extra Y-chromosomed super-butch bastard of a middle prince. "She's still not got over Pater's murder, never mind the slaughter of your two sprogs...."
"Stavros!" shrieked the Queen suddenly, gnashing her teeth and

pulling her hair. "Stavros! Oh my darling little Greek boy! What have they done to you? What have they done! And where are my darling little princes, where have they gone? *What have you done with them?*"

It was some garden party. Rockets exploded in the cloudless night sky. The delicious aroma of baked potatoes, gunpowder and plot toffee wafted through the Buckingham Palace grounds to mingle with a sweeter, sicklier stench of burning human flesh as over two hundred of Britain's few remaining Catholics screamed in agony atop huge bonfires.

"I just wish the old bitch would hurry up and die of grief or something!" hissed the eldest prince through smilingly gritted teeth as he nodded graciously at the passing mob of baked potato munching, plot toffee chewing and bowing, scraping and forelock tugging guests.
"We'll just have to be patient!" woofed his square-headed sibling. "By the way, bro, any news of the puff?"
The heir to the throne grunted. The younger prince hadn't been seen since the day of their father's disappearance in the nuclear fireball that had ripped the heart out of the posh part of London. The rumour was that he'd escaped to Soho where he'd found sanctuary with the mysterious Gay Mafia - the sinister brotherhood of hardened hard-core homosexual hard men who'd gone underground since their failure to turn Britain into a Fundamentalist Homosexual Republic in the last decade of the last century and the first decade of the current one. World War 3 had put pay to that particular little pink pipe dream. With the final destruction of the Catholic enemy, the revenge crazed Queen - driven almost insane with grief over the loss of The Duke and then, a year later, of the two young princes - had dropped all pretence of being a constitutional monarch, re-introduced overt feudalism and declared holy war on all possible opposition to her absolute power. The Gay Mafia's front organisation, New Labour, had, of course, been

one of her first victims.

"Stavros!" shrieked the Queen. "My darling Stavros! What have they done to you?! What have they done!"
"Oh shut up, you stupid old bitch!" yelled the heir to the throne. 'He's dead! Fucking well dead! Do you understand!? DEAD! Just like you'll be soon, you stupid old cow!"

And then the manhole cover at the princes' feet popped open and clattered to the ground 12 feet away with a loud clang.

CLANG!

The garden party hub-bub ceased as all and sundry turned to stare at the hideous apparition that now crawled from the sewers.

"D-d-d-dukey!?" gasped the Queen. "Is that you?"

The hideous confusion of twisted flesh pulled itself up onto the Buckingham Palace lawn and lay there, spasming.

It was revolting.

"Hiiiiiik RAAAAAAAAAAAAAAAAAALPH!" projectile shock-vomited the heir to the throne in disgust.
"Hiiiiiik RAAAAAAAAAAAAAAAAAALPH!" vomited his younger brother in agreement.
"Hiiiiiik RAAAAAAAAAAAAAAAAAALPH!"
"Hiiiiiik RAAAAAAAAAAAAAAAAAALPH!"
"Hiiiiiik RAAAAAAAAAAAAAAAAAALPH!" and 'BLUUUUUUUUUUUUUUUUUUUUUUUUUUUUUUUUUUUURGH!" vomited all the guests in sympathy.
For although the vile beast that twitched, frothed and visibly physically mutated in front of them was recognisably The

Duke, it was obviously a Duke whose semi-reptilian mutant DNA had been completely corrupted by years of exposure to the radiation that still made Kensington and Knightsbridge a no-go-zone for everyone except the slave-driven prole clean-up squads. A Duke whose miraculous ability to heal himself of almost any wound had been hideously and satanically perverted. A Duke who had mutated into some sort of grisly giant cancer-beast which had spent the last three years eating mutated rats and radioactive sewage while it built up the strength to crawl here today.

"Oh Stavros! It is you! Oh speak to me, baby! Say rude things about black Commonwealth leaders like you used to ! I won't mind, honest!" babbled the Queen as she took the stomach-churningly grotesque monster in her arms and hugged it.

"Hiiiiiik RAAAAAAAAAAAAAAAAAALPH!" and "BLUUUUUUUUUUUUUUUUUUUUUURGH!" projectile shock vomited the watching princes and the assembled garden party guests gratuitously as rockets continued to explode in the air above them.

"Urk! Agrooble! Ack!" grunted the feebly flapping Duke-beast as it tried desperately hard to form part of its still savagely mutating lizard DNA into a semi-functional voice box.

"Hiiiiiik RAAAAAAAAAAAAAAAAAALPH!"
"BLUUUUUUUUUUUUUUUUUUUUUURGH!"
Boom! Bang! Fizz! Pow!

"Ack! What - URK! - ho, Queeny! Uk! Sorry to be such a damn nigger in the - AK! - woodpile, so to speak!" gasped the Duke-beast, eventually.
"Oh, Dukey. it's been so sad and lonely without you!" gushed the Queen as the vile monstrosity she cradled in her arms spasmed savagely like the alien monster in John Carpenter's

The Thing.
"Listen up - kak!- old girl!" coughed the Duke. "I've afraid that I've not got long to - urk! - live."
"Oh no! Say it ain't so! Don't leave me again!"
"Stop your fucking - ACK! -blubbing, woman! Pull yourself together, for God's sake! There are - ik! -peasants watching!" yelled the Duke, shrugging her off and staggering to (the hideous outgrowths of seething, bubbling cancerous tissue that had once been) his feet with a superhuman effort of will.
"Yes, yes, of course. You're right, Dukey, you're always right!" said the Queen, rising to her feet and striking a noble pose. "For I may have the weak and feeble body of a woman but my heart is that of a King, nay, not just a King, but a King of England!"
"That's the fucking spirit!" roared the Duke, staggering slightly as he leaked vile black gunk from over two hundred malevolent orifices. "Now pin back the cunting shell-likes, sweetcheeks and listen the - urk! - fuck up. First off: Those two cunts, old Jug Ears and fucking Square Head..." - the Duke grew a savagely twisted pseudo-arm and gestured towards the two still violently projectile shock-vomiting princes - "are still in cahoots with the fucking Pope!"
"But...!" gasped the Queen.
"But bollocks!" rapsed the vile and disgusting monster formerly known as The Duke. "Listen, I've just spent the last 3 fucking years in mortal bloody - ak!- agony lying in radio-fucking-active fucking tampon, dead gerbil and used fucking johnny strewn liquid bastard - urk! - sewage, right? And about six months in I started hearing fucking voices, OK! Fucking - erk! -voices telling me things! Understand!? And one of the things they told me is that those two fucking useless - erk! -toe-rags are still working for the fucking Pope, right? Cos the Pope, right, *isn't fucking dead!!!!!!!!!!*"
"I-I-I-It's n-n-not true! BLUUUUUUUUUUUUUUUUURGH!" vomited the eldest prince.
"Yoiks! It's no good, bro! She's rumbled us! Come on, let's

make a run for it! Hiiiiiik RAAAAAAAAAAAAAAAAAALPH!" spewed the younger one.
"Not so fast, TRAITORS!" spat the Queen.
"Himmler! Diablo! Tebbit! Satan! Thatcher! Ronnie! Reggie! Mao! Mad Frankie! Chaos! Ripper! Liam! Noel! Gummer! Winston! Jarvis! Cerys! Hague! Blair! Pooh! Eeyore! Leonardo! Kurt! Britney! Son Of Sam! Dr. Shipman! Courtney 2! Di! MC Hammer! Trevor! Stalin! Leatherface! Pol Pot! Winona! Judas! Janus! Josey Lawrence! Keano! Stam! Cantona! Norman 'bite your legs' Hunter! Posh and Becks!" yelled the Queenand, with many a happy yelp her elite pack of steel-fanged crack killer corgis came trotting up around her heels.
The Queen pointed a long and bony finger at the cowering princes.
"No, mummy! Please, don't do it!" squealed the heir to the throne, disgracefully pissing and shitting himself.
"Oh don't be such a bloody baby!" laughed the younger prince, deciding to face death with insane bravado, "Oh and by the way, did I ever tell you that I fucked your wife's tiny fucking brains out? Honk! Ha! Yes, the anorexic little bitch said that I made her come in ways that she never knew were possible. Ha! Honk! Yes! I've always hated you, you big eared cunt! Do you know that? Honk! And another thing, I was going to have you bumped off the very minute the old bitch over there died - oh stop crying, will you, it's bloody embarrassing!"
"KILL!" screeched the Queen.
The two treacherous brothers, one blubbing like an incredibly soft gurly and the other stood erect and giving the Nazi salute, disappeared under a furiously yapping tide of killer-corgi flesh.
"One more thing - hack! - sweetcheeks!" wheezed the Duke, slowly collapsing into a pool of bubbling slime.
"Yes, what is it?" asked the Queen regally, steadfastly refusing to let her husband's imminent death shatter her new-found air of icy cool regal dignity.
"The voices...urk!" gasped the Duke, "they...they told me that...ack! .....that...the fucking Papists....aaaargh!....that....that

they'd planted a...aaagh!...a....a...d...doomsday...hak!...a doomsday d-d-d-device under the...the...gak!....p-p-p-p-palace..."

BAKOOOOOOOOM!

The grounds of Buckingham Palace suddenly trembled under the force of a 9.7 on the Richter scale motherandfatherfucker of an earthquake. Huge geysers of molten rock burst through the immaculately manicured croquet lawn. Guest ran insanely screaming in every direction as massive great fissures opened up under their feet. Chaos! Mayhem! Anarchy! Death, destruction and total bloody *DISASTER!!!!!*

"The SS organisation has been constituted, by Himmler, according to the principals of the Jesuit's Order, Their regulations and the Spiritual Exercises prescribed by Ignatius of Loyola were the model Himmler tried to copy exactly...The 'Reichsfuhrer SS' - Himmler's title as supreme of the SS - was to be the equivalent of the Jesuit's "General" and the whole structure of the direction was a close imitation of the Catholic Church's hierarchial order. A mediaval castle, near Paderborn in Westphalia, and called 'Webelsbourg', was restord; it became what could be called a SS monastery."

***Le Chef Du Contre-Espionnage Nazi Vous Parle* by Walter Schellenberg**

CHAPTER 20

"Wake up, bitch!"
Groggily the Queen opened her eyes.
Where was she? What had happened?
Slowly, her head still reeling, she clambered to her feet - and surveyed a scene of utter destruction.
London - the throbbing epicentre of the British Empire - was no more. In its place was desolate landscape of still cooling

molten rock.
"You fuck with my city, I fuck with yours!" laughed the voice.
The Queen turned slowly....and looked straight into the madly staring eyes of....*The Pope!*
"Oh, Your Holiness, what a surprise!" smiled the Queen.
"Let's knock off the pleasantries shall we?" spat the Pope. He was dressed in the pentagram tattooed one-piece human skin cat suit and massive horned helmet of The Anti-Pope Of The Satanic Church Of The Fucking Bastard Anti-Christ. The time for deception had passed. No point now in pretending to be a "Christian". Now, now that so much of the world over which the Brit Royals and the Vatican had fought so hard for so many centuries had been all but utterly destroyed, now he could dress in the regalia of his true calling - that of head bastard of the secret anti-Christian religion that the tax-collector Saul had set up in 33AD in order to suppress the true socialistic teachings of the dangerous revolutionary, Jesus Christ.

"So what happens now?" smiled the Queen, casually.
"Now you die,. bitch!" screamed the Pope, whipping out a Star Wars style light-sabre and leaping to the attack.
"OK!" snarled the Queen, who shook her own light-sabre out of the voluminous left sleeve of her purple kimono, flicked it into life and rushed to meet her evil nemesis.

SHWING!

SHWING!

SHWING!

SHWING!

SHWING!

SHWING!

SHWING!

SHWING!

SHWING!

SHWING!

SHWING!

SHWING!

SHWING!

SHWING!

SHWING!

SHWING!

SHWING!

SHWING!

SHWING!

SHWING!

SHWING!

SHWING!

SHWING!

SHWING!

SHWING!

SHWING!

SHWING!

SHWING!

SHWING!

SHWING!

SHWING!

SHWING!

SHWING!

SHWING!

SHWING!

"AARGH!"

(This page has been left blank so you can use your crayons to draw a picture of the Queen and the Pope having a sword fight.)

The Queen's superbly muscled left arm fell to the floor with a sickening slap.
"Got you now, bitch!" crowed the Pope.

SHWING!

The Queen's superbly muscled right arm also fell to the floor with a sickening slap.
"And now!" frothed the Pope, insanely, "YOU DIE!"
The ground beneath their feet rumbled and shook..
Suddenly a huge crevice opened up just behind the Pope.
"Oh, I'm sorry! Was them your nuts?" quipped the Queen as she savagely booted the Pope in the testicles and then drop-kicked the cunt in the face so that he teetered back, lost his balance and fell right into the sulphur-fume reeking abyss.

"AIIIIIII

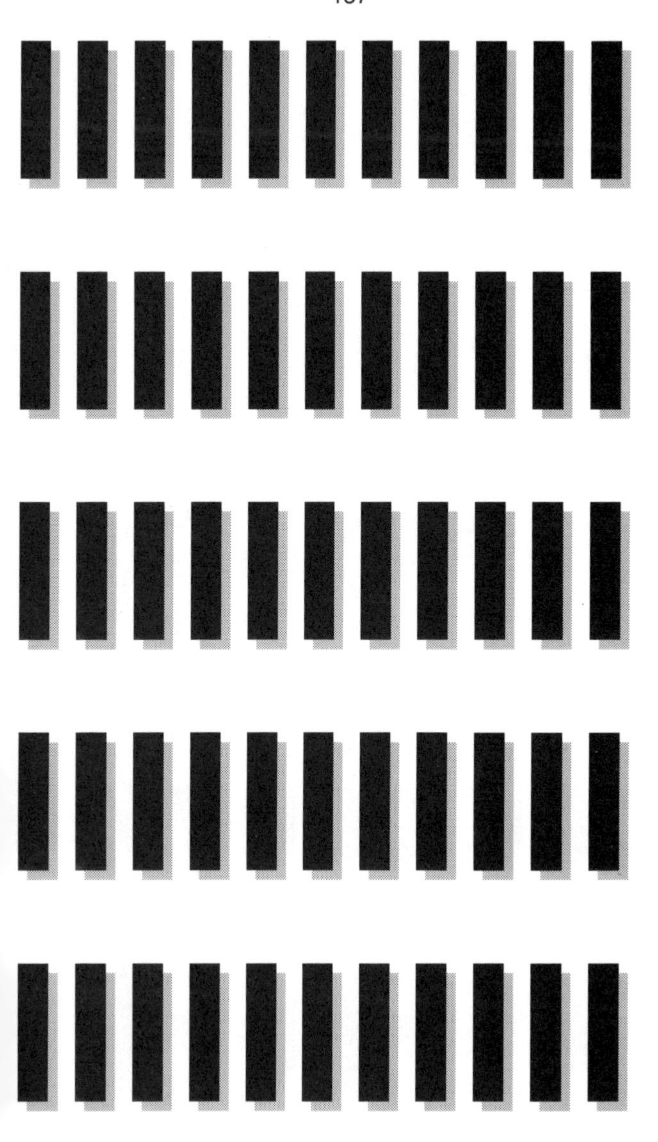

IIIIIIIIIII

IIIIIIIIIII

IIIIEEEEE

EEEEEEEE

EEEEEEEE

EEEEEEEE

EEEEEEEE

EEEEEEEE

EEEEEEEE

EEEEEEEE

EEEEEEEE

EEEEEEEE

EEEEEEEE

EEEEEEEE

EEEEEEEE

EEEEE!"

screamed the Pope as he hurtled to oblivion.
"BYEEEEEEEE!" yelled the Queen sarcastically as she peered over the rim of the bottomless pit with glee.

Right! That was bloody well that! The 500 year war between the British Royal family and the Vatican was finally over! And one had won! Huzzah! OK, so she'd had her arms chopped off but they'd soon grow back thanks to her semi-reptilian mutant DNA. OK, so her entire family had been killed but she wasn't *that* old, she could still breed another one, what with modern technology and that. And, OK, so the world was pretty fucked, what with all the atom bombs and earthquakes and volcanoes and stuff going off but, hell, things could be worse. With a little bit of work and a little bit of luck, fuck it, she'd soon have things ship shape and Bristol fashion again and then - with the Catholic Church finally out of the way - the British Empire would rise again, this time to rule the entire world! For ever! And why should it stop there, thought the Queen, looking up into the night sky. There was a whole galaxy to conquer! And other galaxies beyond that! An Intergalactic British Empire! Well why not? Why not indeed? Like, who the fuck was gonna stop her, eh?
Trembling with blood lust and violently jerking in a demented spastic parody of an E-overdosed tekno-raver's last ever epileptic fit as her semi-reptilian mutant Royal DNA began the slow and incredibly painful re-growth of her missing arms, the Queen tossed back her gore-spattered head and let out the ancient victory cry of the British Royal Family.

“UUUUU

UUUUUU

UUUUUU

UUUUUU

UUUUUU

UUUHAAA

AAAAAAA

AAAAAAA

AAAAAAA

AAAAAAA

AAAAAAA

ARGH!

YOU

CUNTZ!"

And then she laughed her fucking cock off. Metaphorically speaking.

But just then a svelte figure that had been hiding behind a giant stalagmite of still cooling molten slag came screaming towards her with murder in its heart.

“YOU KILLED MR MITTENZ ZZZZZZZ

ZZZZZZZ

ZZZZZ!"

It was the youngest prince, dressed in a fetching lilac one-piece bathing costume and Gerri Spice style stacked platform sandals and still berserk with grief over the murder of the only being he had ever loved and had ever loved him back.

"What the f..*OOF!* " grunted the Queen as the screaming mincer leapt on her back and started flailing away at her head with his puny little fists.

"Shut it, you puff!" roared the still armless Queen as she vainly tried to head-butt the screaming cat-lover the fuck off. But it was no use.

She lost her balance.

And then she and her youngest son, screaming insanely and pissing and shitting themselves in extreme fear, fell helplessly into the same abyss which had swallowed the fucking Pope.

"AIIIIIII

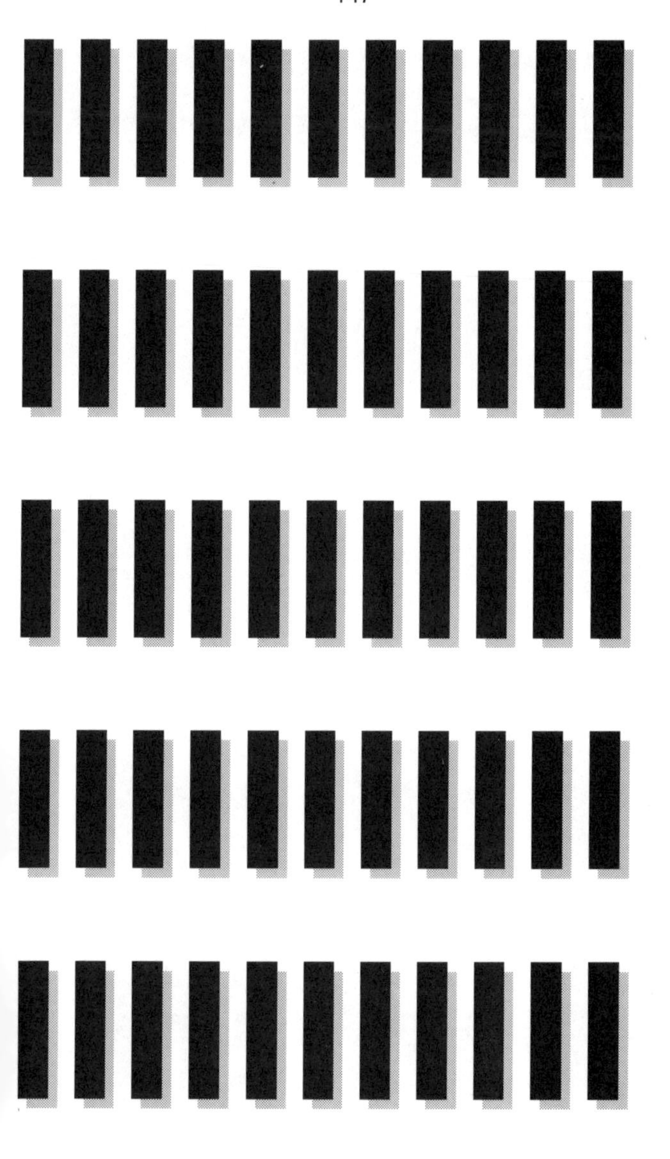

IIIIIIIIIII

IIIIIIIIIII

IIIIEEEEE

EEEEEEEE

EEEEEEEE

EEEEEEEE

EEEEEEEE

EEEEEEEE

EEEEEEEE

EEEEEEEE

EEEEE!”

“Religion is the opium of the people.”

***Criticism Of Hegel’s Philospohy Of Right* by Karl Marx**

EPILOG

As the Queen’s scream finally faded away into nothingness, four horsemen trotted slowly into view.

Jesus ‘Fucking’ Christ.
Vladimir ‘Len’ Lenin.
Leon ‘The Icepick’ Trotsky.
And Wat ‘The Fuck’ Tyler.

They sat, swapped jokes, smoked joints and waited.

Eventually a massive chopped Harley Hog growled into view.

“Jaysus!” quipped the driver, pulling his goggles up and grinning madly. “Would that be your holy feckin self, then?”

“Yes, O’Brian, this’d be me holy feckin self then! “ chuckled Jesus, leaping off his horse and rushing to embrace his cheeky wee Irish lover.
“So it all went to plan then?” asked Jesus suddenly serious.

"Like clockwork!" grinned "Father" Ryan O'Brian.
"And did you sort the new Bible out?"
"Oh yes! And I've got a sample here, so I have." affirmed O'Brian. "Look at this bit. You see, the bit where it said "And all of you who believeth in me shall have eternal life" now reads "All of you muthas who, like, embrace international revolutionary socialism shall have eternal life, presuming that the pigs don't off you in the meantime that is," which. of course, is what you actually said!" grinned O'Brian.
"OFFICIAL!" roared Jesus. And then they all laughed. Conspiratorially. Like mad pirates.

And thus it was that the international proletariat - under the democratically-centrist leadership of Jesus and a bunch of ultra-hard-core proto-communists and bolsheviks that everybody thought had died yonks back but in fact had actually faked their own deaths and gone into hiding instead - rose up and threw of the shackles of imperialism, capitalism, feudalism and religion. And then - after a historically brief period of consolidation during which all the fascists, racists, nazis, bosses, Tories, sexists, homophobes, reactionaries and "serious" novelists were rounded up and shot - they established Heaven On Earth.

And everybody lived happily ever after.

Literally.

THE END

(This page has been left blank so you can use your crayons to draw a picture of the historically inevitable victory of the proletariat.)

GET YOUR COCK OUT

By MARK MANNING

ATTACK!

WHERE THE NOVEL HAS A NERVOUS BREAKDOWN

This generation needs a NEW literature - writing that apes, matches, arodies and supersedes the flickeringly fast 900 MPH ATTACK! TTACK ATTACK! velocity of early 21st century popular culture at its nost mEnTaL!

HARD-CORE ANARCHO-COMMIE SEX PULP

Ve will publish writers who think they're rock stars, rock stars who hink they're writers and we will make supernovas of the stuttering, vild-eyed, slack-jawed drooling idiot-geek geniuses who lurk in the anzine/internet shadows.

HORROR! SEX! WAR! DRUGS! VIOLENCE!

"Subtlety" is found in the dictionary between "shit" and "syphilis".

VICTORY OR DEATH!

he self-perpetuating ponce-mafia oligarchy of effete bourgeois ankers who run the 'literary scene' must be swept aside by a tidal ave of screaming urchin tits-out teenage terror totty and destroyed!

TTACK! ATTACK! ATTACK!

Hail the social surrealist revolution!